IN MY DREAMS

Bless ran through their defenses in her mind. They were strong. And she was a demon slayer, one of the few in the world alive today, she guessed. She whirled in a reenactment of the move she'd done on that yellow-eyed demon. It didn't come off quite the same when she was in the body, but it was pretty good. She kicked and punched to the beat of the music. Yeah, she was Bless, the big, bad, black demon slayer. Buffy, you better watch yo'self, there's a new girl in town. Bless giggled to herself.

"Having fun?"

She spun to the sight of Rick leaning in the doorway watching her, hands in his pockets. How embarrassing.

Her face heated like red-hot coals and she turned back to the dishwater and plunged her hands in. A few seconds later she felt his warm body behind her, his lips at her neck. "You have rhythm, woman. You turn me on."

BOOK YOUR PLACE ON OUR WEBSITE AND MAKE THE READING CONNECTION!

We've created a customized website just for our very special readers, where you can get the inside scoop on everything that's going on with Zebra, Pinnacle and Kensington books.

When you come online, you'll have the exciting opportunity to:

- View covers of upcoming books
- Read sample chapters
- Learn about our future publishing schedule (listed by publication month *and author*)
- Find out when your favorite authors will be visiting a city near you
- Search for and order backlist books from our online catalog
- Check out author bios and background information
- Send e-mail to your favorite authors
- Meet the Kensington staff online
- Join us in weekly chats with authors, readers and other guests
- Get writing guidelines
- AND MUCH MORE!

Visit our website at
http://www.kensingtonbooks.com

IN MY DREAMS

Monica Jackson

DAFINA BOOKS
KENSINGTON PUBLISHING CORP.
http://www.kensingtonbooks.com

1

Bless Sanderson leaned against the hard tile wall of the tiny hospital linen closet, and the dark stranger grasped her in his arms. She didn't feel a flicker of alarm but curled her legs around his thighs and yanked him closer, reveling in the hot wetness of his mouth covering hers.

She'd met the dark stranger many times before.

He eased the blouse off her shoulders. It dropped to the floor, a white wisp in the darkness, forgotten. Then he reached behind her and unsnapped her bra, releasing her full, dark breasts. He feasted his eyes on them, while her nipples hardened in the air-conditioned breeze from the vent above them.

She could hardly wait for his touch. She moistened in anticipation, her groin rolling against his.

He groaned and buried his face in her bra, inhaling her scent. He liked to draw the wanting out—he said it made the having sweeter.

She heard footsteps passing by. They paused outside the door. At that moment, she felt his tongue against her breast, the warm wetness encircling her nipples. The footsteps continued on.

She inhaled, his tongue at her breasts bringing an answering response from her femininity.

"Don't make me wait, do it now," she whispered, sensing the coming of the morning.

Lifting his head, he touched his lips to hers and trailed them across her cheek. "We have time," he said.

Bless swore as the blare of sirens filled the air.

Bless opened her eyes to the harsh ring of her alarm clock, and punched the button with a savage motion. An ache of incompletion settled between her thighs, but if she wanted to get to work on time . . . It wasn't fair. The dreams were coming more frequently, always the dark stranger, his touch, his kisses, his body. Unsettling, unwelcome dreams.

She'd given up on that part of life. When she was younger, she went out and tried men and relationships a few times out of curiosity, but was disappointed or hurt, sometimes both.

In Red Creek, Georgia, the eligible men were few and far between. And her chance of meeting a man who made her pulses race as the dark stranger, well, the possibility was remote at best. She was resigned to her fate and had settled into a state of comfortable acceptance.

Bless observed her cohorts. Most turned to the Lord. The church overflowed with black women, their sexual energy channeled into gospel and spirit, the aisles shaking with the power. It was all good. She was there too, right along with them. She stayed away from the Saturday night bars, the furtive encounters with substandard or married men for the sake of desire. She didn't let her aches flow over into bitterness like some women, eager to slash and backstab any woman who looked like she might be getting something that they could only dream about.

Most of the time Bless was content. That made her doubly upset about this new yearning that she could barely control.

The man who haunted her dreams was tall and well built, intelligent and kind, with a ready sense of humor and a twinkle in his dark eyes. His bronze skin reminded her of caramel. Tickly stubble developed rapidly if he missed a day of shaving over his sexy dimples in both cheeks and his chin. He was the type who cared nothing about clothes, but always looked well put together anyway.

Bless groaned and rolled out of bed to go to the bathroom. Later, she stared at her morning face in the bathroom mirror, pudgy, dark, plain, and topped with a plain relaxed bob that she simply wrapped each night since she couldn't be bothered fooling with her hair overmuch.

Her body matched her face, strong and hefty, a good body for an RN. It wasn't the body of a woman who was well loved, and definitely not the body that would attract someone like the dark stranger. She wasn't built for passion; that was her sister's function.

They joked that Ginger had received all the beauty genes in the family. Ginger was red-skinned with a wild mane of brownish red-tinged hair to match. She had exotic and sultry features, almond eyes, and full heart-shaped lips, a gorgeous face to match a slim, elegant, long-legged body.

Yes, Ginger had the all the beauty, but Bless had something more. The sight. Bless had no doubt that the dark stranger existed. Everyone she dreamed about always did. Bless dreamed dreams, saw visions, heard voices. She had for as long as she could remember.

When she said something about it to her teacher, they sent her to a doctor, who sent her to another and another. Despite her aunt's attempts to intervene, she was diagnosed with almost every vague psychosis in existence. Her aunt finally gave in to the pressure to put Bless on medication, and as she predicted, all it did was make Bless sleepy; the visions, dreams, and voices continued.

She had a happy childhood. The three of them were inseparable back then. Three little girls, each a year apart in age, sisters and best friends, related, yet so different. Ginger was the youngest, the prettiest, the outgoing one, and the one who got in the most trouble by far. Maris, the middle child, was developmentally disabled, functionally able to play and care for herself, but capable of limited communication and learning. Bless was the oldest, quiet, stolid, and reliable. The leader, the one with the power.

She always got along with others, did well in school, had no trouble at home, and exhibited no bizarre behavior. Apparently she was nothing at all like other folk who had delusions, saw visions, and heard voices.

So in a few years the shrinks gave up on her. They rescinded the diagnoses and stopped the medication. Her therapist ignored her when she talked about the visions or her powers. She figured that they decided nothing was wrong with her except that she was a liar.

Bless wasn't a liar, and she knew that she wasn't crazy. Since they had no help for her, they chose not to believe her. It was a hard lesson for a little kid to learn—that you can't always trust the people you're supposed to trust the most.

It was a lesson she never forgot.

Bless slid her ID through the time clock. It was 6:30 A.M., another twelve hours to go and another few dollars to earn. The emergency room was usually quiet in Red Creek. They had the infrequent auto accident or such, but more often Bless dealt with fevers and falls, nursing home residents nearing their end, and anxious parents of children with strange rashes.

Emergency room work wasn't her love. When she was in nursing school, she was drawn to the nursery, the babies. She loved helping brand-new life into the world, devoid of psychic impression. A clean slate, a new start. That was where she wanted to work. But as usual, she put her wants aside and went where she was most needed, and where she could do the most good. This was where the trauma happened, where life slipped away unexpectedly.

Because not only did Bless dream the truth, sometimes she could heal. She glanced at her hands. You'd think power would bring joy instead of . . . her gaze slid away from the door of the linen closet she'd dreamed about that morning . . . instead of duty, denial, and obligation.

But enough of self-pity. Bless put her melancholy mood aside, humming a gospel song as she went to get a cup of coffee.

She was starting on her second cup when a woman burst through the ER doors carrying a baby swaddled in blankets.

"Somebody help, oh God, help me!"

Bless put down her coffee and ran. Mike, the male nurse, was already getting ready to start the IV. The doctor examined the baby on the table. Emma, another nurse, tried to talk to the mother, who collapsed against the wall, sobbing.

Bless glanced at the baby, unconscious and badly burned. As soon as Bless touched the infant, she knew he wouldn't live the next twenty minutes. She put the electrodes in place. The infant was in shock, his vital signs failing, and his heartbeat already starting to become erratic. She covered the baby's skin with gauze doused in saline while Mike got the IV cannula in and started infusing fluids. He pulled the crash cart closer.

Unless Bless intervened now, the baby would soon be gone. She gathered energies from the earth and put both hands on him. It seemed as if the room filled with a green glow emanating from her violet-tinged aura. At first she thought others would have to see it, but she knew now from experience they perceived nothing. She flushed the baby's barely perceptible gray-white aura with life essence and prayed that would be enough. If it was His will, it would be.

"Bless?" the doctor asked. Her eyes snapped open.

"The helicopter is on the way. The only way this child will survive is on a Level One trauma burn unit." The doctor grasped her shoulder. "Sweetie, I know this is upsetting," he said, in what she knew he thought was a fatherly manner, but came off as patronizing. "We'll have a process session over this afterwards. Let's just get through this."

"Thank you, Doctor," Bless said, trying not to roll her eyes at the mention of the dreaded process sessions. During the last one, he made everyone take off their shoes, stand in a circle, hold hands, and confess one way they needed to improve.

She looked at the monitor. Much better. Mike stopped leaning on the crash cart. The baby would make it.

The day was thankfully uneventful after that, but the minutes of her twelve-hour shift ticked away slowly. The sun settled behind the horizon when Bless finally walked into the hospital parking lot, her feet sore, her back sending twinges of pain radiating outward.

Her day wasn't over. Bless pulled up in the McDonald's drive-thru and ordered a salad for herself and a hamburger and fries for her sister. A few minutes later she parked her car in the driveway of the Birchtree Communal Home for Living and rang the doorbell. Sandy, one of the more pleasant counselors, opened the door holding a dish towel. "It's good to see you again, Bless. Your sister is in her room."

Bless nodded at some of the other women in the large house as she climbed the stairs to her sister's room.

The door was shut. Her much more social roommate with Down's syndrome was somewhere else in the house. Maris sat on the bed in a darkened room. Bless turned on the light. Maris didn't blink or acknowledge Bless at all, lost in her own inner world. "I brought you some food from McDonald's. I know how you love their fries." She proffered the bag.

Maris shook herself like someone waking and took the bag, greedily opening it. She tore open the toy first. It was a wind-up figure that lit up and she played with it for a few seconds with delight before discarding it and getting some fries to munch on. Bless watched her with pleasure. Maris seemed always happy. The happiest of the three of them.

Maris straightened and stared at Bless. She never talked much, no more than a monosyllabic word or two indicating her needs. "What's wrong, honey?" Bless asked.

Suddenly a lightning-like flash seared across Bless's field of vision. A baby. Not the injured Caucasian baby in the ER, but a brown baby, staring up at her, from her arms. She looked up and her heart pounded. The dark stranger. Could it be possible? Could the baby be . . . hers? Her heart contracted at the thought. Lightning flashed again and a dark cloud grew over the baby's face. Bless couldn't remove it. She grew frantic. Her sister Ginger's face emerged from the cloud, and the baby and the dark stranger were gone.

Bless gasped. She clutched the sides of her chair, feeling disoriented. She never *went* without warning anymore. She glanced at her sister, wondering if she noticed anything. Maris was eating her French fries, unconcerned. Bless stood and kissed her on the cheek. "Bye, baby. See you in a few days."

Maris waved.

2

Driving home from the Communal Home for Living, Bless pondered her vision, more frustrated by the longing that accompanied it than the content, needing to be satisfied with her lot. This recent spate of lusts and baby longings were wearing her down.

She'd go home and pray about it and hope that would calm her. She had too much to do to spend time fretting and feeling discontent about things she couldn't change. It unsettled her and reminded her too much of Ginger.

She approached the big old farmhouse where her family had lived as far back as she could remember. Their roots were in Red Creek, and Bless loved the place. The country air, the people who knew all her business as well as she knew theirs, the rich red clay, Red Creek was a part of her. She couldn't imagine living anywhere else.

They were constantly updating the old frame house to make it livable. Cheery yellow siding with white trim had been a recent addition, Touching the remote to the garage, she pulled in and un-locked the door to the kitchen. Bless sighed to see the dirty dishes in the sink and food still on the stove. Aunt Praise would cook, but she didn't like to clean up and too frequently left the mess for her neice.

The television was on and Bless walked into the living room. Aunt Miriam was sitting on the couch staring blankly at a golfing tournament. Bless picked up the remote and changed to a cartoon station. She sat beside her and patted her on the thigh. Miriam nodded at the television, probably in appre-ciation. "Do you know where Praise is, Aunt Miriam?" Of course she didn't answer. Miriam was develop-mentally challenged the same as Maris. It ran in the family.

She touched Miriam's hand and lightning flashed. She couldn't credit it happening again, but there was the baby, the dark stranger, and more quickly this time, Ginger. Bless was shaking when the vision faded away and she felt the fabric of the couch under her thighs. What happened next was stranger yet. Miriam turned to her and said, as clear as a hot blue July day, "Go to Ginger now. Go to your sister."

Bless stared at Miriam. She'd never heard her speak two distinct sentences in her life. She started to stutter, then she got the words out, "Why, Miriam? Why do you want me to go to Ginger in Atlanta?"

Miriam turned back to stare at the cartoon on the television, rocking and laughing. Bless wanted to shake her and scream, but she knew it would be to no avail. She stood, her knees wobbly, and went to find Aunt Praise. She needed advice.

Aunt Praise was closeted in her office with a cus-tomer. To earn money, she made charms, did minor spells, and gave psychic readings for the townsfolk. Bless's lips thinned. She didn't approve of such use of the power, much less engage in it.

She tried not to be too judgmental, but Praise's activities brought unsavory types into their home. Not to mention unsavory vibrations. Also sometimes it boomeranged back on them and Bless had to engage in complicated rescue operations her aunt wasn't aware of. She tried to speak to her about it, but apparently Praise didn't discern energies the way she could.

Aunt Praise was stubborn and liked to be independent, and this was the only way she knew to make a living. So Bless had to pick up after her in more ways than one. She was continually cleaning their home of unclean psychic energies. It got tiresome.

Bless went to her room and picked up the phone to call Ginger. A thrill of fear went through her and she found it hard to breathe. She tried to punch in the numbers, but her eyes blurred. That was it. She was going to her sister's apartment in Atlanta tomorrow. Something was going on, something that Ginger needed her help with.

But after a twelve-hour shift, visiting her sister, and the stresses of this day, she couldn't manage the drive tonight. She'd leave in the morning. Bless dropped her scrubs on the floor. She was exhausted. Crawling into bed in her underwear, she was fast asleep in a few minutes.

Lightning. A storm raged over a scorched world. Hordes of demons scurried across the earth eager to seek out and destroy hated humanity.

The machines of war had failed. The world's

armies had fallen. All the weapons of mass destruction—chemical, biological, and nuclear—had failed. Science was completely defeated.

But on the horizon, a light grew. The ones of power gathered to defend the world against the evil that threatened to consume it.

Among them, Glory prepared to fight in the final battle.

She heard a woman's voice, urgent. "Any one of them can turn the tide. Darkness seeks to destroy the ones of power now, while they still can."

By habit Bless woke long before anybody else in the house did. She was profoundly troubled as she showered, dressed, and took her suitcase down from her closet and filled it with the basics. She didn't plan on socializing or partying with Ginger. She hoped she wouldn't be staying long. She packed for ten days.

Sending white light through the house to cleanse it, Bless headed down to the kitchen to start breakfast.

Bacon, eggs, and pancakes were on the stove, coffee was in the pot, and Miriam sat at the table picking at her food when Aunt Praise entered the kitchen around eight-thirty.

"Good morning, Bless, sorry I missed you last night, but I had work." Praise busied herself filling a plate. "Looks delicious. Thank you, honey."

"I need to talk to you," Bless said.

"What's on your mind?" Praise settled down at the table and dug into the plate.

Bless regarded Praise with affection tinged with exasperation. She was getting older, sixty-six years old, although she didn't look a day over fifty. She

IMPORTANT MESSAGE

FOR _____

DATE _____ TIME _____ A.M. / P.M.

M_____

OF _____

PHONE _____
☐ FAX   AREA CODE   NUMBER   EXTENSION
☐ MOBILE _____
   AREA CODE   NUMBER   TIME TO CALL

TELEPHONED		PLEASE CALL	
CAME TO SEE YOU		WILL CALL AGAIN	
WANTS TO SEE YOU		RUSH	
RETURNED YOUR CALL		SPECIAL ATTENTION	

MESSAGE _____

_____

_____

_____

_____

SIGNED _____

Office DEPOT

was the woman who'd raised her, the closest thing she had to a mother.

"I had waking visions with no warning for the first time in years. Both with the same message, 'Go to Ginger now.' " Praise's chewing slowed, and a frown started to develop on her face.

Bless's gaze turned to Miriam, who was looking out the window at a bird. "Last night Miriam spoke to me. What she said was to go to Ginger, go to my sister. Two complete sentences."

Praise didn't look surprised, just took a sip of coffee. "Have you called Ginger?" she asked.

"I can't. I tried twice."

"Stop trying then. Don't go either."

Bless frowned. "Why not? She could be in trouble—"

"More reason not to go. There's history in our family."

"I don't care about the past. The key word is 'family.' She's my sister and she may need my help. I'm calling her now." Bless stood and crossed the room to the phone. She picked it up and a heavy, oppressive dread filled her. She started to press the numbers and that dread turned into panic. She hung the phone up on the receiver as fast as if it had turned into a poisonous snake in her hand.

Praise watched her. "See what I mean? Leave it alone. We sisters have history, I told you. Sometimes around the age that you're at, it can be dangerous if we're in proximity."

"Dangerous? That's ridiculous. Ginger and I have squabbled at times, but we're sisters, and that's normal. We've always basically got along."

Praise shook her head. "Please don't go."

"There's nothing you can say. I've packed my bags. I'm leaving for Atlanta within the hour."

Praise sniffed and wiped her eyes. "At least let me make you a charm for protection."

"Aunt Praise, you know I don't like those things. There's another thing, I also had one of those apocalyptic dreams."

Praise shrugged. "One good thing about those dreams is that the scale is generally too big for you to worry about doing anything but enjoying the show."

"I suppose you could say that was the case," Bless murmured. "I better get going." She glanced at Miriam as she left the room and was surprised that Miriam met her eyes with her lips curved in a smile.

Bless tried to call Ginger again in the car on her cell phone, but that feeling of dread and oppression happened. A spell?

Bless hated spells, especially when they happened to her, and generally, spells couldn't happen to her. A spell has to have a gate, a weakness. A person had to have knowledge that a spell was being cast on them, belief in the spell, and fear of the spell. Bless had none of these things. It was very strange. Ginger might need her protection after all.

Bless pulled on the highway before she punched in the numbers to call the hospital to tell them that she'd be gone for a while. If they didn't like it, tough. She had family business to take care of. She put her foot on the gas and rolled over the asphalt toward the big, bad city of Atlanta.

Bless and her sister had an interesting relationship, one of those sibling relationships where there was both love and active dislike.

She couldn't imagine anybody more opposite from herself than Ginger. Ginger was one of those little girls who'd steal from the collection basket in church, smile in the preacher's face, and buy everybody candy afterward.

In high school, Ginger was the head of the meanest and most stylish clique of girls in school. She wasn't around after that because she swore that after she graduated, all Red Creek would see of her would be the dust her hind end kicked up as she got the hell out of there, and she wasn't lying. Ginger didn't even stick around to collect her diploma.

But they stayed in touch. Bless was fixed in Red Creek, the town as much a part of her as her skin. Ginger was like the wind, was always searching and going hither and thither. Despite their differences, Bless understood Ginger's emptiness the way no one else could. Bless wished she could soothe her, but there was no way to heal discontent.

She didn't want trouble to come to her sister, but she sensed terrible trouble indeed. The inside of the car was warm, but Bless shivered as if a cold wind had passed. A bad omen.

3

A hundred or so miles away in Atlanta, Rick Jensen was worried. Swank was out of jail. Rick's brother, Malik, had disappeared with enough of Swank's money that Swank's first priority would be getting his hands on his brother's girlfriend, Ginger, to find out where Malik had gone.

The only thing that stopped Swank so far was the amount of surveillance that Rick put on Ginger. But the department was far more interested in bringing Malik to justice than protecting Ginger. The fact that Malik had made off with hundreds of thousands of dollars that would have gone into the city coffers upon Swank's arrest did not set well with the department. With every passing day, Malik's trail grew colder and the pressure on Rick increased to take the resources he was using on Ginger and use them elsewhere.

His time was running out and he'd about had it with Ginger. He'd wanted to relocate her to a protection program before Swank got out of jail, but she flatly refused. So he had to spend way too much of his free time with her. It was a trial, because Ginger got on his last nerve.

Also, he didn't want his family too involved with his brother's girlfriend. His brother had told the family nothing about her, and probably with good reason, because when he met her, he instantly knew his mother and sister wouldn't take to her. Why did his brother choose a woman so different from the women who'd raised and loved him? Rick didn't understand it.

But he owed it to his brother to keep her safe and he'd do the best he could. His gut feeling told him that Ginger knew something about where Malik was hiding. He bet his brother was lying back on some white-sand beach with some disgusting drink with an umbrella stuck in it while Rick was taking care of his business for him.

It was the same when they were kids. Malik would jump into deep doo-doo and Rick would pull him out. Dad kept him in line with his iron fist, but once Dad was gone, Malik veered way off the straight and narrow.

Rick saw the way he was sliding, and warned him about trying to live within one's means and working for one's wants. Malik never did pay him any mind. High-maintenance women such as Ginger and flashy cars were the name of the game to Malik, along with constant business schemes and money-making deals on the side. It was only a matter of time until the right opportunity came, Malik would joke, and then he'd settle in the Caribbean and write the great African-American novel.

If you don't get yourself in big trouble first, Rick would quip back. He always thought that Malik was basically all talk and no action. And then this crap happened. He was going to especially wring Malik's scrawny neck for saddling him with Ginger.

Bless was anxious to find out what, if anything, was going on with Ginger, so she was relieved to see Ginger's classic red MG in front of her apartment. She slid out of her sensible white Toyota Tercel and rang the doorbell.

"Hang on," she heard her sister yell.

Ginger pulled the door open. Bless gasped, but neither said a word. Ginger stared at Bless, and Bless stared at Ginger's stomach.

Finally Bless asked, "May I come in?"

"Uh, sure."

Bless followed Ginger to the living room, marveling at Ginger's hugely swollen abdomen, her ungainly waddle, her thickened thighs, and were those *jowls* under Ginger's chin? She didn't mean to be uncharitable, but she'd never seen Ginger in any state that was short of dazzling. She was shocked.

"Won't you sit down?" Bless said this instead of Ginger. She couldn't stand to see her sister on her feet, looking as if she was panting, a moment longer. Ginger seemed as if she was going to fall over.

Ginger sank into a recliner, picked up a hand fan, and fanned furiously. "This being pregnant is worse than the devil." She waved Bless toward the kitchen. "If you want something to drink, go help yourself. And bring me a Michelob."

"Should you be drinking alcohol?"

"Why don't you bring me my beer now and hold the lecture for later."

Bless bit her lip. She supposed one beer wouldn't hurt at this late stage, but still . . .

"Sorry. I don't mean to be impatient with you, sis, but your sudden presence is surprising," Ginger said, trying to adjust her bulk in the recliner.

"That's all right." Bless went into the kitchen and rummaged in Ginger's refrigerator, shaking her head at the lack of nutritious food, and got out a diet cola for herself and a beer for Ginger.

Bless handed Ginger the beer, popped the top on the cola, and leaned back on the couch. "Well? Why no word about your pregnancy? You look like you're at least eight months," she asked.

"Almost nine." Ginger shook her head. "You know I never wanted a child. I couldn't find a doctor who'd do a tubal on me years ago." She pointed at her stomach. "This happened despite being on birth control pills, using a condom, and applying spermicidal cream all at once. Then after I missed my period, I was desperate enough to take an overdose of those morning-after pills. Amazing, isn't it?"

"Astounding," Bless said in a dry voice.

"But that's not all. I tried to get an abortion, not once but several times. Despite the procedure being legal, and me having the cash, I was thwarted at every turn,"

"What do you mean thwarted?"

"Thwarted, as in prevented. For instance, this silly fool started waving around a gun right before the thing was supposed to be sucked out." Ginger started feeling around the sides of the recliner and pulled out a cigarette case.

"I knew it was all for show and nobody was really going to be hurt, so I told them to go ahead and finish," she continued as she lit the cigarette.

Bless gave a pointed cough.

"But they all wanted to panic and shit," Ginger said, ignoring Bless's cough.

Bless stared at her sister, speechless.

"Yeah, I was *too* pissed because at least that time I'd made it to the clinic. When I tried to get there the first time, my car blew up. Then my taxi blew up." Ginger flicked the ashes and shook her head. "I took the goddamn bus and it went off the curb. Finally, I decided to walk. I got nearly run over, cars jumping curbs to get at my ass. Sparrows kamikazed me and pigeons divebombed me with pigeon poop. Folks who didn't know me from Adam tried to drag me off the street. I had to turn around and go back home covered with pigeon shit and skid marks on my ass."

"That sounds thwarted all right," Bless managed to get out.

"Tell me about it," Ginger agreed.

"So, I take it that you're not thrilled about the prospect of motherhood?"

Her sister cocked her head and stared at her. "Ya think?" she asked, looking disgusted.

Bless tried not to chew her fingernails. This was a bit much. She heaved a heavy sigh. "Have you considered simply letting someone else raise the child?" she asked.

Ginger leaned forward. "You know that won't solve the problem."

Bless made an exasperated sound. "I'm not understanding you at all. What problem?"

"I'll die if I have this goddamn baby. That's the problem."

Bless reached out to touch Ginger's stomach. The baby was healthy. Ginger was healthy, and she saw no precursors of maternal disaster. "You're not going to die in childbirth," she said. "You know that I know."

Ginger picked up the beer again. "You don't get

it, do you? I'm not talking about childbirth. I'm talking about us, our family. The brood mare always dies young. Look what happened to our mother. Our grandmother."

Bless drew in her breath, held it, and let it out real slow. "That's silly superstition, Ginger. You can't stake your child's life—"

"Because of the weird shit that's gone on around us since we were infants? It's always the same. There's three sisters. One is fine and popular, one is weird and homely, and one's an idiot. The fine one has three girls, and then she had to pay because she's well and truly fucked. She kicks the bucket, and the homely sister raises them. It's the same generation after generation. It never changes. We're not real people, we're just rats stuck on a fucking fatalistic treadmill, and I want off."

Ginger sniffed then took a huge drag on her cigarette and blew a cloud of smoke toward Bless. "I don't want to have a bunch of brats and die in a few years. I was having dreams that there was a chance to change it now for some reason, but everything I tried . . . failed."

She blew out another cloud of smoke. "Maybe you're here for a reason. I know you have power. Maybe you're here to help me get rid of it once and for all."

Bless was too busy coughing to answer.

Bless didn't say much to Ginger after her tirade. At least now she knew why she had the pressing premonitions that she needed to get here ASAP. She wondered why the universe took so long. Her sister was ready to deliver the child soon and had obviously not bothered with prenatal care at all. She appeared to be living on candy bars, diet coke, and beer.

Bless has taken refuge in the kitchen, saying she wanted to cook dinner and tidy up. Ginger was sitting in the living room laughing at some horrendous reality show on television. She wondered how Ginger supported herself. She was a hairdresser and she didn't see how Ginger could manage all the standing required.

It didn't seem as if the father was in the picture, but that was no surprise. Men went in and out of Ginger's life through a revolving door. Ginger made no bones that the measure of a man was the heft of his wallet combined with the size of his penis multiplied by his skill in bed.

Ginger was nothing if not direct. Men had a certain purpose in her world, and if they failed to fulfill it, they could hit the road as far as she was concerned. This seemed to make her more, not less, popular with men. They certainly loved a challenge and Ginger was certainly that. No man had conquered her yet.

Bless looked through the cabinets. She wouldn't be able to cook until she bought some food. She picked up the phone to order out. She settled for a pizza with extra toppings and triple veggies. Probably more nutrients than Ginger had had for weeks.

She hung up the phone feeling sick. This place was rank with darkness to the point of foulness. Ginger was hell-bent on murder. You can't have intentions like that and not funk up the psychic atmosphere. Bless drew white light from the heavens and flooded the apartment, but it barely made a dent.

Once Ginger figured out that Bless was as determined to prevent infanticide as she was determined to commit it, there'd be a showdown. Bless flipped through the yellow pages looking for a grocery that delivered. She found one and mentally noted it. Let Ginger bring it on. Bless wasn't budging an inch.

Waves lapped around her and the dark stranger, as they lay entangled on the sand. Twilight blue was the color of the sky and the ocean, the evening ocean breezes balmy. She knew that she'd recently been satiated. He'd filled her with loving to the brim. She was disappointed that she'd missed it. The ocean lapped at them lovingly and cleansed any evidence of their union away.

If this time would only last forever.

"Forever is now, and yesterday and tomorrow. For us, time is meaningless," the dark stranger said.

Bless didn't think she'd said it out loud.

He touched his lips to hers. They tasted of salt. Her heart filled to bursting. Maybe she didn't have to say what she felt. She loved this man and he loved her. She didn't know where they began or ended, but she knew that.

"See?" he whispered. "You only think you don't know me now."

"You look pretty good for somebody who hasn't gotten laid since time out of mind," Ginger murmured absentmindedly while she read the morning paper.

Bless thought that Ginger was treading on dangerous ground commenting on folks' looks, good or bad, since she definitely wasn't at her best herself lately, but Bless wisely decided to keep her opinions quiet. Her feelings still stung after Ginger had described her as "weird" and "homely" last night. It might be true, but Ginger didn't have to throw it in her face.

Ginger lit up a cigarette and Bless flinched. If she knew Ginger, there was no point in asking her to lay off the cigarettes around her. In fact, it would make it worse.

"So how are your powers doing?" Ginger asked. "Still crazy with the voices and visions after all these years?"

"Occasionally."

"You said you could heal. Anything else?"

Bless bit her lip. She felt reluctant to talk to Ginger about what she could or couldn't do, and anyway, she wasn't fully sure herself. "I can heal sometimes. When the Lord wills it."

"You are always so preachy. What about your will? What do you want? You ever want anything for yourself, Bless?"

An image of the dark stranger came to mind and she lowered her eyes.

Ginger gave a low laugh. "There's something you want. But you're not telling. I want to know something. Since you can heal, doesn't it work in reverse? You could drain the life force from someone, couldn't you?"

Bless looked straight into Ginger's eyes. "No, I couldn't."

"You could if you wanted to."

Bless shook her head. "No, I couldn't," she repeated, her voice soft.

"So what are you going to do to help me get rid of this?" Ginger asked, and getting straight to the point indicating her swollen belly.

Bless sighed.

"It's not my function to help you get rid of the child." Bless got to the point also. She was going to eventually have to, and it might as well be now.

Ginger stared at Bless and chewed her bottom lip as she digested this.

"Well, you need to get the hell out of my apartment then, because getting rid of this thing is my main 'function' and interest right now," Ginger said.

"No," Bless replied.

"What did you say?"

"I said no."

Ginger's face twisted in amazement. Bless would have laughed if the situation wasn't so serious. She bet Ginger had never heard Bless say no directly to her face in her life.

"What does that mean?" Ginger finally asked.

"Do you need a dictionary?" Bless asked.

Ginger's mouth dropped open.

At that moment somebody banged at the front door. "Let me in, I have groceries," a man's voice called.

Bless went to the door, pulled it open, and stood aside. A tall man staggered through, obscured by the large sacks of food he was carrying. He dumped everything on the kitchen table, where Ginger was sitting.

"I looked in your refrigerator the other day," he said by way of explanation. Then he turned to Bless.

It was the dark stranger.

She gasped. All the blood rushed from her face down to her feet and back up to her head again. She thought she was going to faint and swayed a little. She blinked too fast and breathed too slow. She put her hands behind her back and gave herself a secret little pinch. No, this wasn't a dream.

4

The dark stranger held out his hand to Bless.
She grasped it tentatively, half expecting a bolt of
lightning at most, or electricity at least. But his fingers
were firm, cool, and impersonal. "My name is
Rick," he said.

She shook his hand. "My n-name is Bless," she
managed to answer. "I'm one of Ginger's sisters."

A big grin spread over Rick's face. "I'm pleased
to meet you. I was hoping some of her family
would show up to get this girl straight. I work long
hours, so I'm not able to make it over to check on
her as often as I like."

Bless sank into a chair, not trusting her feet to
bear her weight. He must be the father. Disappointment
crashed down on her like an avalanche of
stone. She didn't understand. It made no sense.
How could he be Ginger's lover, *and belong to Bless
also?* Every fiber of her body knew it.

"My sister was just leaving to go back to Red
Creek," Ginger said through stiff lips.

"No, I'm not leaving. I'm staying here until

Ginger delivers and I'll be staying for a good while after to help out. I'm an RN."

He beamed at her. "That's just what she needs."

"Stop talking about me like I'm not here! Get out! Get the hell out of my apartment before I call the police!" Ginger yelled at Bless.

Bless ignored her and reached for the groceries to take to the kitchen.

Rick flinched, and then reached into his jacket and took out his badge. "Did you forget that I *am* the police? Detective Rick Jensen, at your service. And what may I ask is the problem?" he asked Ginger.

He ducked at the ashtray that Ginger threw at his head.

Bless grasped a sack of groceries in her arms and headed for the kitchen. "Come along with me and pay her no mind," she said to Rick. "Ginger and I never did get along well, and I think with the stress of this unplanned pregnancy..." Bless touched her temple with her index finger and revolved it in the universal sign language.

Rick nodded in understanding.

"You goddamn bitch, if you don't pack your shit and get out of my house, I'm going to—"

Bless dropped the sack of groceries back on the table and swung around. "What are you going to do?" she demanded, her hands on her hips.

Ginger sputtered, no words emerging, her face contorted with anger.

"I didn't think so. You can't do a thing. Now go and sit down somewhere while I unpack these groceries and put on dinner."

Ginger wheeled and marched out of the living room. A moment later the door to her bedroom slammed so hard the entire apartment shook.

Bless picked the bag of groceries back up and headed for the kitchen. Rick picked up another bag and followed her.

His name was Rick and he was a cop, a detective, Bless thought. How ordinary. How could he be so familiar to her? She knew how he tasted, the contours of the most intimate parts of his body. She knew what hurt him, and she knew what made him happiest. She knew him better than she knew anybody else. But did he know her? Was she a part of his dreams?

"Have we met before?" Bless asked him. "You seem familiar."

"I don't think so," he answered, without missing a beat.

Bless turned away to put cans in the pantry, feeling disappointed. But what did she expect? He was her sister's man, and the father of her sister's child.

Maybe she had the dreams because he was the first man who was sexually attractive to her that she would get within ten yards of during the next ten years.

Whatever the case was, she needed to pull her head together. She had to suss him out, and find out what he knew about Ginger's murderous intentions toward the child. More importantly, what were his own?

"It's good you brought the food. I was shocked when I saw how poorly she'd been eating," Bless said.

"So was I." He stood beside her and helped put the dry goods on the high shelves. She liked his easy competence with domestic chores. But he was standing too close. She could smell his familiar scent, a light, clean-smelling aftershave. It made her want to lean toward him and sway against his hard body, feel his strong arms around her. She needed him. This was so difficult.

To her dismay, her eyes filled with tears and they spilled over her cheeks.

She tried to turn away and reach for a paper towel before he'd notice, but it was too late.

"Let me," he said. He took a clean, soft dish towel and wiped her face, his fingers deft and tender. "Want to talk about it?" he asked.

Bless shook her head. "There's nothing to talk about. I—I guess Ginger upset me more than I thought."

"She was very harsh." He leaned back against the sink and regarded her. "Are you sure it's worth staying here? Ginger's a big girl. Bottom line, she's an adult and she can take care of herself."

"I know Ginger's more than adept at taking care of herself. But it's not Ginger I'm worried about." Bless started to pace. "Has it been like this her entire pregnancy?" Bless asked.

"I think so."

Bless waited for him to say more, but apparently that was it.

"I'm worried about the baby." She shot a glance at him. "Aren't you?"

"Well, I guess so, but I see that as her problem."

Bless frowned. He didn't seem like one of those trifling, irresponsible, no-good, dirty, doggish lokes who spread their seed all over creation yet take no responsibility for their issue.

"So I take it that you don't feel the father has an equal responsibility?" she asked.

She must have looked dangerous because Rick got fidgety. "Sounds like you have opinions about paternal responsibility," he said.

"Strong ones. But I'm trying to have a civil conversation with you."

"Whatever your opinion of a father's role, Ginger is going to have to carry the burden. That's just the way it is right now."

Bless breathed in and out real slow. It helped her to remember that she was a Christian woman and it wouldn't be a good thing to go upside his head, because she was so angry. It also helped her not to hyperventilate and pass out because she could barely tolerate the emotions swirling through her. Having the dark stranger in front of her in the flesh was surreal. It made reality feel like a dream. It made her wonder, even when she wanted to slap the tar out of him, when he was going to reach out for her and make everything all right. "Ginger doesn't want the child. She never wanted the child," Bless said in a rush of words.

"Yeah. It's a real mess."

Bless's fingers curled into fists. "Is that all you have to say? I can't believe you don't give a damn! You—you anal opening!"

Rick stared at her. "Anal opening? That's a new one," he muttered, shaking his head. "I don't see why you're so upset at me. As soon as I can find my brother, we'll straighten things out."

"Your brother?"

"The father. He's been missing for a few months."

Bless blinked rapidly.

"You thought I was the father, didn't you?" he asked, instantly jumping to the right conclusion and making her feel worse.

Bless nodded, embarrassed.

"We just met. I suppose it's a reasonable assumption if your sister didn't tell you anything."

He looked away. "She never mentioned my brother?" It was more of a statement than a question.

"No, she didn't." Ginger waxed poetic about the men in Atlanta. The number and variety she enjoyed was astonishing and the poetry mainly had to do with their masculine endowments and how accomplished they were at using them. But she never mentioned an exclusive relationship. Bless didn't think Ginger was capable of an exclusive relationship with a man.

Rick looked dismayed at the realization of her sister's depth of feeling, or lack or it, for his brother. She wanted to kiss the expression off his face. How was she going to deal with this man if she couldn't talk to him for thirty seconds without wanting to touch him?

"It was mighty good of you to leave your home to come to Atlanta to help out your sister," he said, his words deliberate. "Especially seeing how unappreciative she is. I was hoping that it's the pressure of my brother being missing on top of her pregnancy that sent her into a depression. I offered to get her help, even offered to pay for it, but she refused. Now you tell me that she's like this all the time, that she can't even get along with her own sister." He sighed, looking sad.

She wanted to tell Rick that she'd said they didn't get along to account for Ginger's bad behavior at the moment. That right now she and Ginger were at odds because of the baby and life-or-death stakes, but over the years, when it came down to family, they usually defended each other's back. They were opposites, but Ginger made her laugh with her outrageousness. She said things that Bless could only think. She did things that Bless could only dream. And Bless knew that she grounded Ginger. She was Ginger's touchstone, the place her sister fled to for balance and stability when things were spinning out of control. They completed something in each other.

She didn't excuse Ginger's behavior, but she could understand it. It was Ginger's survival instinct kicking into high gear peppered with liberal doses of narcissism. She had more than enough of that, and the girl didn't have the maternal instinct of an alley cat. But Ginger never pretended to be something she wasn't. She would have been happily sterilized if she could have gotten the procedure done.

"Ginger's all mouth. She isn't all that bad," Bless said. "You're right about most of her behavior being stress-related." She folded the paper grocery sacks and stored them under the sink. "What happened to your brother?"

"He works with computers, a computer geek combined with this thug swagger. Women came easy for him, but not Ginger. She was a challenge and he loves a challenge. Everybody else thinks he ran out on Ginger, abandoned her. But I never saw him so happy as when he found the pregnancy testing kit Ginger had purchased. He told me he was going to buy her a ring."

Bless caught the phrase "everybody else." So did he think his brother was hiding out somewhere waiting for Ginger? Was that the reason Ginger was so desperate to get rid of the baby?

"He found the pregnancy testing kit? You mean she never told him?"

"Not yet. She hadn't gotten to it yet. She was out and he found the positive results of a pregnancy testing kit in her bathroom when he came home from work unexpectedly one day. He didn't say anything to her. That's when he called me." Rick ran his hand over his face in pained memory.

"Apparently he never told her that he knew of the happy news or gave her the ring. We found evidence that he did purchase the ring. Then he was gone."

The last of the groceries were put away, and the silence that settled between them in the kitchen was awkward.

"I'll see you again soon, Bless," Rick said. He touched her hand and there was that electricity she had expected when she first met him. It radiated through her body like a shiver. She wondered if he felt it too. His eyes dropped and his fingers touched hers a little too long. Then he turned, and with a few strides of his long legs, he was out of the kitchen, out of the apartment, but not out of her life. He was so much a part of her she could holler.

5

Rick was worried that Ginger's sister had come to town because it complicated things more than they already were. He nodded to one of his men watching Ginger's apartment. He slid behind his steering wheel and got on his radio, calling in Bless's auto tag, and the make and model of her car. She'd need to be tailed.

He didn't know how he'd be able to protect both of them. At least Ginger was staying close to home. He had a bad feeling about this. He was worried about his brother. And he wanted to throttle his brother's silly girlfriend about her nonchalance over the child his sibling was so excited about.

Bless was a breeze of fresh air. Calm, sensible, she'd get Ginger straight. He'd been dismayed when he saw how badly Ginger treated her, but Bless took it in stride. Bless, unusual name, for an unusual woman.

She wasn't beautiful at all in the traditional sense, but her face suited him and he'd been drawn to her. Her features were regular and pleasing and

her skin was smooth, unblemished and fine tex-
tured as the richest chocolate. Her chocolate eyes
were beautiful, big, with full lashes, soft, sweet, but
full of wisdom and strength. It was amazing how
much you could get from a person's eyes. He
wanted to drown in hers.

Her mouth was even better. Full cinnamon lips
that were meant to look freshly kissed. She had the
perfect body for his tastes, a woman's body with
full breasts, lush thighs, and a bottom that could . . .
his thoughts threatened to wander into treacherous areas. The best thing about her was how he felt
around her. Calm and peaceful, even when his
emotions obviously were unsettled as hers were.
She made him feel he belonged by her side. He
spied no ring on her finger. He didn't know how
he could stand it if she belonged to someone else.
But it didn't bother him, because he knew she
didn't, didn't know how he knew, he just knew. Bless
was one woman that he was going to get to know
much better.

His eyes narrowed as he figured out the solution
to his dilemma of how to keep them safe. The solution he didn't think of before now seemed perfect with Bless in the picture.

He was going to level with them and get them
out of that apartment first thing in the morning.
He'd bring Bless and Ginger to his place until
things cooled off. They were family of a sort now.
How could he let something happen to Malik's
only child? He'd be better able to watch over his
brother's crazy girlfriend and figure out where he
was.

* * *

"Is he gone?" Ginger said, walking into the kitchen sniffing.

Bless had cooked a down-home Southern dinner of fried chicken, mashed potatoes, green beans with ham shanks, and flaky biscuits with yellow pound cake on the side. The peach cobbler was for dessert.

Ginger's eyes widened when she saw the food. "There goes my figure," she muttered.

"What figure?"

Ginger patted her swollen belly. "You have a point." She eased into a chair. "I guess I'm not surprised you're still here. You always were stubborn as hell."

"So are you."

"One of a kind."

Bless turned with a sharp look and Ginger giggled. Bless laughed with her, and the tension of the last two days drained away back to the way things used to be, when despite how much they got on each other's last nerve, they were friends.

It lasted until after dinner. Ginger pushed her plate away, reached for a toothpick, and leaned back in the chair. "You know, sis. If you help me, you help yourself. You can't want to live a sterile, sexless life raising somebody else's kids. I know you want your own family, your own man, white picket fence, and all that shit. Maybe now you can have it." She leaned forward with an intense stare. "I've been having dreams. Strange dreams. And I never have dreams I remember. Something tells me now is the time things can be different, now is the time we can change things and get off the fucking treadmill."

"Why are things different?" Bless asked.

"Because of the timing, I think. It's time for something."

Bless thrummed her fingers on the table, musing on her sister's words. It was true the pattern of her family members' lives was a strange and coincidental one. But it was also true that every cell in her body rebelled against the causing of death in any way, shape, or form. Whichever way Bless twisted or turned to looked at it, the bringer of death also brought darkness.

"I work with the light," Bless whispered.

Ginger frowned at her. "What does that have to do with anything?"

"It has everything to do it. You want me to bring death, work with darkness." She sighed. "You know, Ginger, when there's something I don't understand, that's bigger than my comprehension, I've always gone by a simple guideline."

Bless helped herself to another piece of cobbler. "Stick to what you know, what feels right. I make decisions based on my principles, the foundations of why I do what I do. And what I do is work with the light. You want me to move over to the darkness. It ain't happening. You savvy?"

Ginger took a deep breath and exhaled. "Damn, girl, the world isn't black and white. It's colored in shades of gray."

Bless shook her head. "My world is what I make it and I make it real simple."

"So what are we going to do?"

"I don't know what you're going to do, sister. But what I'm going to do is clean up this kitchen and go to bed, get up tomorrow, and deal with what the day brings. Like I said, I don't try to make my world hard."

Bless stood and took their plates to the sink, rinsed them, and put them in the dishwasher. Ginger watched her for a while, sighed heavily, and got up. A moment later, Bless heard the sound of a laughter soundtrack coming from the television in the living room.

The serene lapping of the waves against the hull belied the agonies inside. The smell of human waste mixed with decay and death. There was little sound. Voices were a rarity. To take the energy to talk, to groan or cry, you needed hope. Hope had fled this place. These people waited to die and willed it to come quickly for they sailed on a boat of ghost demons, bound for the tortures of hell.

Three little girls huddled by their mother, their tears long ago used up. Their mother gathered her will and strength for one last act. One thing she could do for her daughters. Her throat worked and her voice emerged, husky and rough. Heads rose, turned to see, and lowered again.

Her children crept closer to her, trying to merge with her, somehow sensing that she was leaving. Her voice went on and on, ebbing with her life, until she was silent.

The next morning when they found her dead, the three girls were huddled beside her, unmoving. They had to physically pry them away.

But the powerful spell for the sisters to live and to never be separated came to be. But not as the mother had hoped.

A feminine voice whispered, *"There are always three, generation after generation. One with beauty, one of power, and one who appears to have nothing at all."*

Bless sat straight up in bed, a fine sheen of sweat covering her skin. She lifted her knees and buried her face in her hands. An image of the mother's face burned behind her closed eyelids. More images—the mother's smile, the mother's touch. A wave of grief came over her, and she sobbed.

Bless inhaled with a hiss as she pulled open the door to Rick's beaming face. He handed her the morning paper and sniffed the air. "I smell coffee. May I come in?"

Bless stood aside, although she really wasn't steeled for Rick in person after a night of erotic romping with his dream alter ego.

She followed him, her gaze dropping to his flexing buttocks. Me oh my, what was she going to do?

He got himself a cup and poured himself some coffee. "Is Ginger around? I need to talk to you both," he said.

"She's still asleep."

He looked relieved. "Maybe I'll tell you first and you can help me present it to Ginger in a more palatable way."

Bless generally tried to limit herself to one cup of coffee, but whatever Rick wanted to talk to them about seemed to make it a two-cup morning, so she poured herself a refill.

"I told you yesterday about my brother, Malik, and how he disappeared with a lot of money. What I didn't finish telling you is that the man who Malik took the money from was released from custody recently. You can imagine how badly he wants to recover his funds. Malik is gone without a trace, but it's well known that Ginger was his girlfriend."

Bless sipped her coffee looking thoughtful. "If it was the case that Ginger knows where Malik is, why hasn't she joined him already?"

Rick pointed to her abdomen.

"The baby." Was that why Ginger was so desperate to get rid of the pregnancy? Was the man who
threatened Ginger the darkness she saw hovering
over her sister and the child? Bless shivered a little.
But Ginger's fear seemed so much bigger than
that. She was afraid of actually having the baby, not
being encumbered by it. But still . . .

"What do you think she should do?" Bless asked.

"I think she needs to get out of here quickly. I've
been able to have her watched and protected so
far, but I don't know how much longer I'm going
to be able to do so in this location."

"Where do you want us to go?"

"My place."

Bless set her coffee cup on the table so fast and
hard that it overflowed. "You must be joking."

"Not at all. You all are family of a sort. I have a
vested interest. I want to keep Malik's child safe
and I want to find my brother. To be perfectly
frank, if anybody has an inkling of where he is, it
would be Ginger."

"I would need to be with my sister her entire
stay. It's very important."

"I agree. I think you'll be an excellent buffer to
keep her from driving me totally insane," Rick said.

Bless gave him a sharp look. His face was straight
and serious.

"If you need a buffer that badly . . ." she started to
say.

He grinned at her and her heart flopped over.
And what he said next made it a thousand times
worse. "What I need is you around."

Bless stared at him, her mouth drying. He shimmered before her eyes and looked as desirable as

an icy bottle of Coke to a woman stranded in the
Gobi Desert.

"I can handle Ginger," he continued. "But we
need to persuade her to move today, and travel
lightly."

6

Getting Ginger to agree to move over to Rick's house was a lot easier than Bless thought. He limited her to two suitcases, and in a couple of hours Bless was following Rick's dark blue SUV down the highway.

He lived closer to the city in an area reclaimed and gentrified. She followed him to a neighborhood of quiet tree-lined streets with renovated homes and town houses with well-kept lawns. She noticed, though, from the children playing and the people walking down the streets that the neighborhood still seemed predominantly black, unlike what Bless had seen before in her travels through neighborhoods renovated to this level.

He pulled up to a wrought iron gate and it swung open. Bless followed him into a circular drive in front of a large brick home. "Malik never told me his brother was the one with the cash," Ginger said with a touch of resentment.

"From what Rick tells me, Malik is the one with the big cash now," Bless quipped. She had enough to worry about; this issue with the babydaddy was peripheral, she sensed. She wanted Ginger to come clean and tell Rick what the real story was.

But Ginger stared out the car window at the house and said nothing.

Rick carried in Ginger's two bags and Bless handled her own. When they got into his foyer, Bless whistled at the expanse of white and immediately wanted to slide out of her shoes. She looked around for furniture and saw none. Rick's house was expansive and empty. Apparently they both looked puzzled, because he said, "I never got around to furnishing the place. However, there are the basics, beds, tables."

He picked up the bags. "Let me show you where your rooms are."

Bless couldn't have asked for a more perfect setup. Her room adjoined Ginger's so she had the advantage of being able to keep a close eye on her sister and yet have privacy too. They shared a bathroom. Her room was simply furnished with a full bed and a bureau.

Rick set the bags inside the door. "This is where my family stays when they show up. I'll give you the grand tour."

There was a table in the kitchen, a huge-screen TV in a room with big pillows on the floor. She peeked in his room and saw a comfortable bedroom suite with a king-size bed. Apparently he liked to spread out. There were four bedrooms.

A lovely house, far too large for a bachelor. What she liked best about it was the vibes. There was no tinge of psychic discord, or if there ever had been, it had faded away. It was a mellow home, as clean and uncluttered in a psychic sense as in the décor.

Bless glanced at Ginger from the corner of her eye. Too bad it wasn't going to stay that way. "Why don't you help me start lunch?" she asked.

Ginger shook her head. "No, give me your car keys. I need to go and get some sort of recliner delivered. How am I going to watch television? Do you see me heaving myself up and down off those floor pillows in this state?"

Ginger did have a point. "Do you have that kind of money?" Bless asked.

"Would I be bringing it up if I didn't?" Ginger said.

"Let me go get my purse."

"You don't have to go, just give me your keys."

Bless just looked at her,

Rick got his keys. "Ladies, I'll drive."

"I didn't expect you to have to chauffeur me," said Ginger.

"How do you propose to get the chair home?"

"I was going to have it delivered."

"You'll have to wait. This way you pick it out and we can bring it in right away."

There was no arguing with that, so they followed Rick out the door.

Bless had a bad feeling about going to a busy mall with Ginger, instead of a stand-alone furniture store, but her sister insisted.

As soon as they got through the doors streaming with busy preholiday sale shoppers, Ginger disappeared into the crowd. "Don't let her get away," Bless yelled at Rick, and took off in the direction that she last saw her sister.

She narrowed her eyes, seeing the rainbows of auras, looking for the unique texture and feel of her sister, opening to find . . . the baby.

It was if she slammed into herself. The baby had

a fully formed presence, separate from Ginger's once Bless extended her perception to feel it. The baby was viable now, a person. She didn't know how she knew the child's name was to be Glory; she simply was sure of it. Bless thrilled in the silvery lavender threads of the new auric vibrations. The baby left a trail as if silver glitter dust drifted from it.

Bless hurried and followed the trail to a fitting room in a menswear store. She pulled open the door without hesitation, feeling somewhat relieved when indeed there was Ginger instead of some half-dressed man. "New taste in clothes?" she asked.

Ginger jumped about three feet in the air. "How did you find me?" she almost yelled.

"Ma'am?" the salesman asked.

"We're busy," Bless said, and thankfully he decided to leave them alone.

"I followed you," Bless answered, deciding now was not the time to go into the more esoteric details. "I told you I wasn't going anywhere and I meant it. Let's go get the chair and go on back to Rick's. He's waiting on us."

"Why don't you just leave me alone?" Ginger moaned. "Go home to your beloved Red Creek. This is none of your business." Tears started to run down Ginger's cheeks. Bless had seldom seen her sister show such open vulnerability, but the stakes had grown too high for her to be moved.

Glory shifted and Bless grasped Ginger's hand and held it to her swollen stomach. "Feel her? Her name is Glory." Ginger snatched her hand away as if burned. "She's the reason this is my business," Bless continued.

"Let me go. It can change everything for us. Our destinies. We change our destinies for the first time. Don't you feel it?" Ginger's whisper was low, fierce.

"Ladies, we're going to have to ask you to leave unless you plan to purchase something."

The salesman had returned with a security guard to bolster his resolve. "We were just going," Bless said to the salesman. "You first," Bless told Ginger, who raised her chin and sailed out of the store. Bless gripped her forearm. "Let me go!" Ginger said.

"Not hardly. I don't feel inclined to go running after you again. You do realize that wherever you go, I'll find you."

Ginger said nothing.

They stepped on the escalator, and when they stepped off, Rick was standing in front of the furniture store, hands in his pockets, tapping his foot. "Where did you go?" he asked as they approached him.

"Please take us back. Ginger's not feeling well. You can come back and get the recliner. Anything big, overstuffed in blue." Blue was the color of protection and heaven knew that was needed.

Rick didn't complain. She knew he wouldn't. He wasn't the complaining type.

Much to Bless's relief, Ginger went off to her room in a sulk. Bless didn't think she could deal with much more. Her nerves were stretched to the thinnest thread. There was too much to this situation she didn't understand. It was like swimming in the ocean in the dark, not knowing where the sharks were lurking.

* * *

Rick walked around several blue recliners, not sure which one to choose. He hated to shop. He also didn't like to feel indecisive, and that was happening on several levels. He had this incredible woman under his roof and no idea of how to make the next move. Rick had never quite been in this dilemma before.

He pulled out his cell phone. His heart predictably quickened as her honey voice answered the phone. "Don't cook," he said. "I'll bring something home."

Maybe he was finally ready for domesticity. He had the big house. So many women's eyes lit up when they first saw it. It was the house that he and Sharon were to live in. Her family had money and she didn't want to wait until he could work up to a place like this. It was her dream home.

She was diagnosed with pancreatic cancer just two months before they were to be married. He wanted to go ahead with the wedding, put a ring on her finger. She wouldn't hear of it. She died nine months after the diagnosis, in this house. She made him promise that he'd marry, fill this house or another one with children. She wanted him to be happy.

Was he happy? He guessed so. He didn't have anything to complain about; he went through the motions just fine. But nothing had mattered since Sharon, and then he met Bless. Something about her blew the cobwebs from his mind. She didn't remind him of Sharon at all, except the way she made him feel. There was something right about her.

He dated, but the women never made an impression. Many were sweet, many tried hard to impress and most were nice enough and definitely attractive enough, but there was something about Bless, even though he hardly knew her. She simply fit him the way no other women did. Women could be like a pair of shoes. It didn't take long to know whether you had the right fit—they either fit, or they didn't.

Bless made him feel as if he had slipped his feet into a pair of just-right house shoes—comfortable, soft, warm, and a perfect fit.

But with Ginger around, it seemed as if they were swimming against a strong river current, trying to keep afloat. He sensed undercurrents between the sisters that he had no knowledge of. He wanted to get to know Bless without the impediment of Ginger. He needed to get her away from the house, and spend some time together, just the two of them.

7

"You have the hots for Rick," Ginger said out of nowhere.

Bless looked up and her eyes narrowed. "Whatever do you mean?"

"I see the way you watch him. As if you're a stray dog and he's a meaty ham hock."

"Please."

"Don't deny that you want him. Honey, I know it's been a while for you in the sex department. I'll be happy to give you a few pointers, free of charge."

"Don't bother—"

"That's all right, we're family. I know it must be hard. Sometimes a woman needs a man's loving, and you've never had that, have you? Well, first thing, why don't you lighten up on the cooking and take some turns around the block when you get up in the morning? Say around ten or twenty. You could stand to lose forty–fifty pounds."

Bless flipped the pancake carefully, her hand

trembling a little. "I don't need your advice and I don't want to hear any of it. I'm fine the way I am."

"You may think so, but you never have had any men knocking on your door to get in, and I do mean that in a literal sense. You should listen to me." Ginger yawned, picked up a slice of bacon, and turned to leave the kitchen. "Call me when you have breakfast ready," she said.

Bless was so mad, she could have cried or slapped Ginger. The latter would have made her feel better but she had to keep calm.

Ginger was getting worse. Bless didn't know how she was going to stand staying with her the few weeks until she had the baby, and afterward, how was she going to manage to keep the baby safe? She knew Ginger wanted to drive her away. This wasn't going to be easy.

"Good morning," Rick said as he entered the kitchen.

His presence did nothing to lower her blood pressure. The dreams had intensified. Having him around in the flesh was like an itch that couldn't be scratched. She'd never been in this state before, one open, throbbing area of sexual need. Ginger had it about right with the meaty ham hock simile. One look at him and she wanted to salivate.

"Morning, Rick. Can I make you a plate?" she asked instead of drooling.

"Please do, it smells great."

She piled his plate with bacon, grits, scrambled eggs, and pancakes. "There's some fruit salad in the refrigerator, want some?"

"This is fine for a start. I haven't ever eaten this good. You're going to fatten me up, woman."

His words were light and teasing, but they caused a pain on that raw area. Was Ginger right? Did he think she was fat?

"Maybe I should start cooking lighter. I could start cooking diet entrées. I could use some help in that area," she said, patting the generous curve of her hip.

Rick actually looked alarmed. "Please don't. You look wonderful, I like a woman with some curves, and diet food is nasty. You're one of the best cooks I've come across in recent memory. This is blasphemy, so don't tell her I said this, but you could give my mama some competition in the kitchen."

Bless smiled at him. He likes a woman with curves, huh? Be still, my foolish heart, she admonished, because she swore it was about to leap out of her chest with joy.

"Have you eaten?" he asked. "Please join me. I want to ask you something."

"I ate earlier, but I'll join you." Bless poured a cup of coffee and settled down across from him.

He leaned toward her and sniffed.

What was up with that? She'd showered this morning. She quelled an impulse to raise her arm and sniff up under it.

"You smell so good. What are you wearing?" he asked.

Bless looked at him, eyes wide. What was she wearing? Soap, deodorant, lotion. "Nothing special," she said. "Just lotion."

"I like the scent."

"Thanks." She made a note to buy out the warehouse, as she struggled against offering him the opportunity to smell more of it. *How about a whole body experience, baby?*

This wasn't like her at all. Bless sipped her coffee. She was going stone crazy over this man.

"What I was wondering is if we could get away next Friday night and spend a little time together alone? Do you like jazz? I was thinking we could have dinner at this jazz club I know with live music and a nice atmosphere."

Lord help her. Somebody needed to come and mop her up off the floor right about now. Could it get any better? Oh yes, she decided as a dream memory of their hot, sweaty bodies tangled together flashed across her mind. It could get a lot better. "I love jazz," Bless said.

"It's a date then."

"Why didn't you tell me that you had breakfast ready?" Ginger demanded, waddling into the kitchen.

Bless closed her eyes in pain. How could she leave that heifer, 'scuse, her sister, alone for an evening? She couldn't. Ginger would be gone and she didn't know if she could locate her again across miles. Bless would either have to cancel the date with Rick or take Ginger along.

With Ginger's presence, the atmosphere in the kitchen changed. Rick had his head in his plate and his eyes on the morning newspaper. Bless started cleaning the kitchen feeling conflicted and depressed when a few moments ago she'd felt like singing.

Bless put down the book she was reading and sighed. She heard the television in the other room and Ginger cackling along with the laugh track. Bless watched television only rarely. She generally was too busy with working, and her days off were filled with errands and things to do. When she got some downtime, she relaxed with music or a good book, or went to see a movie. She'd never had this much downtime in her life before and she was getting bored out of her mind.

She was starting to wonder if this worrying about Ginger's baby wasn't simply stress related for the both of them. Ginger's man had disappeared and Bless had to face how much she craved a child of her own.

Maybe she was feeding into a mutual pathology. Maybe what they both needed was therapy. Or maybe she could get Ginger to agree to a stay at one of those high-end benign mental health facilities where you got to ruminate on your troubles endlessly while being entertained and therapeutized at the same time. She could keep an eye on Ginger in that sort of enclosed environment too. That could be ideal. She had excellent health insurance; Ginger, being pregnant, could get Medicaid; and with her determined intent to kill her child, she certainly qualified for mental health care.

But Ginger wasn't the type to tolerate being among a whole lot of white folk. She didn't know many white folk who'd put up with being isolated with a whole lot of black folk for very long, but they hardly ever took into account the stresses black folk go through all the time in the same situation.

People had different ways of dealing with the stress. On one extreme of the continuum were the loud sort with accentuated Ebonics and chips balanced precariously on their shoulders. They generally were out of their element and acutely uncomfortable. The other end went the Condi Rice route and out-whited the white folk. They generally were raised around white folk or trained for this sort of thing from infancy. Most average folk drifted on one side or the other of this continuum.

Black folk had to be higher functioning than white folk to function within their higher-end facilities. Ginger would certainly be cussing folk out and telling them about themselves, which wouldn't do, even if well deserved. The probability was high that Ginger would be transferred quickly to a less desirable facility. Since she was an RN, Bless knew what that was like and silently crossed the mental health system option off her list.

So that left regular outpatient therapy. She'd look into it, because she was bored out of her mind, she was getting ready to turn down the man of her dreams, and if you stood back and looked at it, the whole situation was getting a touch weird.

Bless picked up the yellow pages to look for a referral to a progressive, female African-American therapist with a New Age bent. Maybe somebody along the lines of Ilanya Vanzant.

Aunt Praise might have some ideas. Bless reached to pick up the phone when it rang.

She wasn't too surprised to hear her aunt at the other end. "It's good to hear from you." She missed her aunts and Red Creek.

"You too, Bless, but you sound worried. Is Ginger doing any better?" Bless had filled her aunt in on Ginger's pregnancy and an overview on her state of mind, leaving out the more graphic details, during a telephone call the night before.

"Not really. We're maintaining the status quo. Time seems to be moving real slow."

Praise sighed. "I have something to send you. It's real important. They called me from the Home. Maris was speaking."

Bless sat upright in the bed. "Really? What was she saying?"

"I went right away. She was in some sort of trance, saying the same thing over and over for hours. I wrote it down. As soon as I got it down correctly, she stopped."

"What was it?" Bless's heart pounded. She had the feeling that whatever it was, it was absolutely vital that she know.

"I'll overnight it. You'll get it tomorrow morning. And Bless . . ."

"What?"

"Be careful, baby. Things aren't as simple as they look on the surface."

Bless hung up the phone. She had a feeling the situation was going to grow much, much weirder and somehow therapy wasn't quite the answer.

Skin on skin. Feverish, hot, and wet, saturated with the scent of sex. She curled her fingers into Rick's shoulders as he withdrew almost to the point he was no longer inside her. Her vaginal muscles contracted trying to draw him deeper inside. So good. The moment stretched out to a point of trembling pleasure. She moaned. The sound broke the thread, and he plunged deep inside her, filling her. It pushed her over the edge where the storm waves battered against the cliffs again and again and again.

Bless awoke, spent. She felt sore, as if she'd actually made love. The stickiness between her thighs had the characteristic musk of man sex. What was happening to her?

She rolled out of bed and headed to the shower. If she was going to remember this sort of dream so vividly and have what appeared to be physical aftereffects, you'd think she'd remember the entire dream and not just pop in for a few moments. At least this time she got in on the best part. But this was getting frustrating to say the least. What was Rick's role in her life? What could she do to make the dreaming either stop . . . or become reality? Bless finished adjusting the water temperature and stepped under the shower.

She'd not got her clothes on when the doorbell rang. Aunt Praise's package! She heard Ginger and she hurriedly pulled on a robe.

Bless made it into the living room in time to see her sister starting to open the package. She darted to her and snatched it. "What is wrong with you?" Ginger asked.

"This has my name on it, not yours," Bless said, and retreated to her room, closing the door.

She hesitated before she opened it. *This will change everything.* Her finger trembled as she ran it along the fold to tear it open. She pulled out a single, unlined piece of paper.

One has beauty, one has power, and one seems to have nothing. Three turns the circle until the end of the age. One of the three breaks the circle either with fear or love. The line either finishes to naught or joins with the light at the Final Battle.

8

Bless stared at the words over and over until they blurred. Lines and circles? But combined with her apocalyptic visions, the prophecy was fairly straightforward as prophecies generally go. She wasn't crazy about the insinuation about this being the end of the age, which was a scary thought.

One of the three breaking the circle with fear was pretty clear—that would be Ginger killing the child—but how was she to break the circle with love? The object of her affections was present, but what did that have to do with it?

Bless couldn't figure out any connection between knocking boots with Rick, as sweet as the thought was, to the Apocalypse. She knew it would be good, but bringing on Armageddon was *way* too extreme. Bless fell backward on the bed, giggling somewhat hysterically at the thought.

Ginger stuck her head in the door. "You okay?"

Bless had the presence of mind to roll over on the prophecy. She had a strong feeling that it was important that Ginger not see it. She grinned up at her sister. "Nope, I'm not okay. I'm still here with you, aren't I?" she answered.

Ginger rolled her eyes and retreated. The basic boundaries of respect and sisterly friendship that she'd always shared with Ginger were wavering, being replaced with something else. She wasn't sure what, but they weren't getting along at all.

She remembered the vision where Glory stood alongside the others facing the coming onslaught and shuddered. Bless never gave the power much thought. It was something like being able to draw or sing well, present and useful, but a part of you that you soon learned to take for granted.

She'd never tested the extents or limits of her abilities. How would you fight? She'd been a fan of Buffy, but unlike the show, with the scrawny blond vampire slayer kicking the crap out of various monsters every week, she knew that the struggle wouldn't be physical, because the threat wasn't physical.

Demons weren't monsters lurking to tear you from limb to limb. The monsters that did looked exactly like people. Supernatural evil attacked the mind and the spirit body.

So how did you fight that? The word "break" implied action against resistance. She stood on the side of the bed and saw in that special way that took in more than was evident to the physical eyes.

Waves curved through the air, everywhere, all sizes, shapes, and colors. They were radio waves, cell phone waves, transmission waves of all sorts arcing through the atmosphere.

She looked at her hands and perceived the glow of her aura, saw the sheen of the psychic residue of the house. She flinched as she saw the ugly viscous black sludge oozing on the floor from the direction of her door. She reached out to touch it and recoiled. Pain and degradation, hatred and fear. It was a residue of pure evil. What was it doing here, so close to her?

Bless put fear aside and said a brief prayer. She pulled open the door to follow the trail. It grew thicker across the living room, repelling the white light Bless sent toward it. She followed it to the den, where the television blared, where her sister sat ensconced in her blue recliner, remote in her hand.

The blackness swirled and enveloped Ginger, almost blocking the glow of her aura. Bless must have gasped because Ginger turned her head and lowered the remote. "What's up with you?" she asked.

Bless, her mouth dry, could only point.

Ginger pointed her index finger at her chest also. "Me? What did I do now?"

"Don't you feel it?" Bless asked.

"Feel what?"

Bless swallowed. "The evil," she said.

"What evil are you talking about? If I didn't know you better, I'd think you been taking a few too many puffs on those funny cigarettes."

Bless thought she'd been doing a good job of controlling her fear up to then, but two yellow slitted snake's eyes appeared in the miasma along with the faint echo of a laugh.

She was back in her room with the door shut between her and it before you could say "pee my pants."

That was what she almost did. Bless discovered that scrambling to the toilet took some drama off a situation and gave her time to reflect on her next move. She connected with the elemental energies and flooded her rooms with all the protective power she could muster.

She still looked around cautiously before leaving the bathroom and holing up in her bedroom. Bless sat on the side of the bed and chewed her lip. Ginger was bad enough, but the tag-along demon might put a damper on the jazz-club date with Rick. *Oh, you don't mind if I bring my sister and her big, black, yellow-eyed demon, do you?*

How long had it been present? Bless remembered the rank atmosphere when she'd first walked into Ginger's apartment. Possibly for a while. Bless hadn't extended herself or her powers since she'd been here. She rarely did, even when healing.

So the demon had been hanging around biding its time . . . for what? What was its purpose with her sister? Often they possessed people, but Ginger was under no direct control because Bless would have sensed that immediately. Ginger was being influenced and that had to happen under some sort of invitation.

Bless sighed. All she really knew about demons was that it was terribly hard to get rid of them once they took up residence. And her sister's purpose was infancide; that would coincide with demonic interests nicely. Her job of protecting Glory had gotten much, much more difficult.

Bless pulled out her cell phone and called her home phone in Red Creek. She exhaled in relief when Praise answered the phone. "I received your package," Bless said.

"Interesting, wasn't it? It made my skin crawl when Maris was intoning that prophecy over and over."

"If you want your skin to crawl, why don't you drive to Atlanta? Ginger has a demon."

"A demon?"

"I saw it with my own eyes."

Aunt Praise was silent. "Did she summon it?" she finally asked.

"I don't know. I doubt it. She seemed unaware of its presence."

"I wish I could tell you to come home right away," Praise said. "But I know that wouldn't be the right thing to do. You decide what you need to do and I'll help you however I can."

Bless's hand clenched the receiver. She consciously slowed down her breathing. Saving the world and demon battle were more than she particularly wanted to take on. She closed her eyes and an image of a brown baby girl and the beloved face of a man danced behind her. Her desires were far simpler and earthier.

"Bless?" Praise asked.

"Yes, I'm here."

"Sometimes you don't get to choose. You're chosen."

"Thank you, Aunt Praise." She clicked off, and sank onto the bed. She pondered on staying in Atlanta versus turning tail and heading for Red Creek. If she stayed, she'd have to confront the demon eventually and in all probability that would mean she'd lose her life. She had no illusions about that. Her mind sifted through possible alternatives.

What if she dragged Ginger to the nearest Catholic church and tried to get her exorcised? Didn't they have specialists in this sort of thing?

Her intuition told her that she probably wouldn't be believed, assuming she could get Ginger and the demon to go to Mass. She also knew she was chosen to deal with this.

Bless moved to the full-length mirror on the back of the bedroom door and studied herself, dark, plump, sporting a short pageboy, and decidedly unglamorous. She was no Buffy. She wasn't the least bit excited about having to kick demon butt.

Lightning played across the mirror and Bless frowned. But she tried to quell her fear and watched.

The small dark figure in the distance was familiar. Was it herself? No, it was Glory. Glory was standing still in the physical plane, clad simply in blue jeans and a sweater, surrounded by a halo of light.

But her other body was in the other place, free of gravity and time, fighting with bolts of her intentions, tearing the demons to shreds with the essences of energy while she writhed and twisted, blocking and eluding their deadly beams. Others joined her. Some died with incandescent flames burning their physical bodies to ash, their light eradicated.

The images faded to Bless standing in front of the mirror, arms clasped around her stomach and looking as sick as she felt.

Bless fretted until the time that Rick was supposed to get home. She badly wanted to get him out of this house, but that posed complications, since it was his house.

The demon hadn't manifested in any way at all and even kept its funky atmosphere confined to the area immediately around Ginger. It was apparently biding its time, but that didn't mean it couldn't change at any moment. It had no problem showing itself to her when it knew she was discerning it.

Although a demon couldn't or wouldn't kill Rick directly unless it took on flesh, it could cause his death and many other unpleasant things. Demons preferred to toy with humans rather than directly cause death. They liked to cause negativity. Demons didn't want to end the world as much as they wanted to control it and make it their playground of endless pain and despair.

Death is man's release. A demon would rather cause a man to beg for death and it would withhold that mercy. But Rick was a cop. He must be in close proximity to all sorts of misery, and demons feed off misery. For a demon to influence a person, there must be a weakness, a gate.

Once the demon is perceived, there's the opening. She had to keep Rick from perceiving the demon at all cost. Since demons never wanted to be perceived by humans, as long as things remained as they were, Rick should be safe. The key being as long as things remained as they were, which of course they wouldn't.

She and Ginger would have to go back to the apartment. They needed to leave as soon as possible, ideally tonight. She wouldn't let Rick be caught in the cross fire.

Bless believed she could protect him against small-time drug gangsters, but if she couldn't, demons rarely appreciated outsiders stepping into their territory. Ginger had far less to fear from them than the demon.

She heard Rick's key in the door. She took a deep breath and left her room. She met Rick at the foyer with a forced smile.

"It's nice to come home to your smiling face," he said.

"Let me get you a drink and you can relax. Hungry? Would you like a snack?" Bless asked, following him into the house and casting a nervous glance at the den.

"We're going to have dinner at the club a little later tonight, aren't we? I could use a snack."

"Why don't you settle down in your bedroom and I'll bring you a glass of beer and something to eat on a tray?"

"Join me?" he asked.

"I will," she said and watched him walk down the hall to his room whistling a tune.

There were only a few rooms with furniture. If they sat around the kitchen table, the prospect of food would bring Ginger running. The only other place was his bedroom, where he could stretch out on the bed and watch the evening news. She could talk to him in privacy too, because his bedroom was one place that Ginger wouldn't invade.

She had some substantial topics to discuss. First, that they really needed to cancel their date, and second, that she and Ginger had to leave his house tonight.

9

Bless narrowed her perceptions as she fixed an appetizer tray. She did not want to see any yellow-eyed demon. She prepared a very large tray of chili con queso dip, buffalo wings, celery, blue cheese dressing, pizza wedges, potato skins sprinkled with cheddar cheese and bacon bits, along with two very large mugs of icy cold beer.

This was not going to be a wine, cheese, and fruit conversation.

She tapped on the door with her foot, her arms laden. When Rick pulled the door open, his eyes widened in appreciation at the food. "By the time we get through all this, we will be far more interested in conversation and music than eating tonight."

She eased the tray on to the bed between them and set his beer on the bedside table. There was no place to sit but on his bed, so she perched on the edge, holding her own beer to her chest like a shield.

"I wanted to talk to you about going out tonight. I don't think it's a good idea."

His eyebrow shot up. He picked up a chip and dipped it in cheese. "Why not?" he asked, before he brought the chip to his lips.

"We shouldn't complicate our relationship. Sometimes things get confused when you muddy the waters. I'd like to remain friends and—"

He pushed the tray to the side, took the beer from her nerveless fingers, and set it beside his on the end table. He sat close beside her and took her hand, entwining his fingers with hers. "The whole point is to get to be friends, Bless."

Her mouth dried and her carefully rehearsed speech evaporated. Gone. She couldn't remember a word. Something about muddied waters and clear running rivers.

He moved, so he was facing her profile. "I can't think of one good reason why we shouldn't get to know one another better. Can you?"

She could think of plenty. She turned her head and opened her mouth to say so, but her gaze caught his and she was lost in it.

His lips moved to cover hers for the first time, as they'd done countless times before in her dreams. His lips were smooth and firm and his touch was like she came home. He gathered her to him and tears ran from under her lids. Lord, it had been so long.

His kiss was hungry and she met it with equal appetite. Her mouth opened and his tongue danced with hers. It wasn't enough. The feel and scent of him in the flesh were like a rising storm. The power and sweetness of it.

She fell back on the bed and he covered her neck and throat with kisses. His touch inflamed her. She moaned and whispered his name. He shifted his body to cover hers with his own . . .

"Bless! Where are you, sis? Bless! I'm hungry."

Bless closed her eyes with something like pain. Ginger couldn't find her in here. She gave Rick an apologetic glance and rolled off the bed.

"Be back soon," he said.

Her heart dropped out of her chest, lay on the floor at his feet, and thump-thumped, bleeding away. That's how hard it was to walk away from that man.

She entered the kitchen and saw Ginger standing in front of the refrigerator, wearing a housedress.

Bless wanted to squint to look at her, but as long as she kept the focus of her perception narrow, like everybody else's she supposed, she was all right. Although she knew the demon was there, she didn't see it, so it didn't affect her.

"I'll make you a snack."

"Rick said y'all were going out tonight. I decided to go with you. I'm tired of being cooped up. Do you have anything to wear?"

"This was supposed to be me and him. We're not going anymore anyway."

"We can't have that. We have to go out. I was counting on it," Ginger said, pouting.

Was the demon counting on it too? She heard the whisper of a snicker, and focused her mind firmly on snacks. "Do you want buffalo wings?" she asked.

"I don't have anything decent to wear in this buffalo silhouette I'm sporting. Do you have anything you can lend me?"

She never thought she'd live to see the day when Ginger asked to borrow her clothes. Her eyebrows shot up. "You want to partake of my humble wardrobe?"

Ginger rolled her eyes. "Don't rub it in. Something red if you have it. And buffalo wings sound good."

She left the kitchen trailing black effluvia, the demon sitting on her back grinning. Bless shuddered. Knowing Ginger, she'd raise hell until they went to the club as planned. Rick was too polite to refuse to take her.

Bless sighed. Her red velvet pantsuit would certainly never feel the same after she knew it was sat upon by a demon. What exactly *do* demons excrete, she wondered?

The jazz club was intimate and cozy, the music soft and mellow. A perfect place to get to know someone. Rick had seemed nonplussed when Ginger bounced up to the passenger seat of his SUV in that red velvet pantsuit, but as Bless predicted, he acted the perfect gentleman.

Ginger was slurping down strawberry daiquiris like soda pops. "It's sort of boring here. Why don't we go to a fancier club? I'm in no shape to party, but at least I can watch."

"Why don't you order?" Rick suggested. "The catfish is great and they grill a mean steak."

He knew just what to say to distract her sister. Ginger picked up the abandoned menu and studied it while Rick motioned for the waiter. "We're ready to order," he said.

"I'll have the catfish," Bless said.

"And what do you want, Ginger?"

"This sixteen-ounce T-bone, rare, all the fixin's. And another daiquiri."

"I'll have the catfish too," Rick said.

Bless had never in her entire life observed her eternally dieting sister eat like she'd been eating lately. Ginger wasn't eating for two; she acted as if she were eating for an army. And that weight she'd put on wasn't coming off magically after she had the child like she seemed to believe.

"Is the baby moving much?" Rick asked.

"What?"

"I asked you if the baby was moving much? Bless told me it would be a girl. I bet you were excited to see it on ultrasound. I know my sister was. She showed those pictures around for weeks and all they looked like was light and shadow to me."

"What ultrasound? And yes, the little bitch moves too much. She needs to keep her ass still so I can sleep." Ginger drained the dregs of her daiquiri with the straw.

Bless doubted if it was possible for a man to be more shocked than Rick was right then. He didn't spend very much time with her sister at all.

Apparently, years of police training kicked in and Rick schooled his features. "How do you all know the baby is a girl if you had no ultrasound?" he asked. Bless guessed he decided to ignore Ginger's choice of terms of maternal affection and focus on something he could understand.

Ginger motioned to the waiter and pointed to her empty glass. The waiter nodded and hurried off. "Do you really need another?" Bless asked, hoping to change the subject.

"Yes, I do believe I really need another." She focused on Rick. "They are always girls, silly. We can't have anything but little girl brat bitches. If things go to plan, I'm to have three, one right after another, pop, pop, pop, like li'l watermelon seeds. Then a few years later, I'll die under mysterious circumstances. That's the way the circle turns."

The way the circle turns. Goose bumps rose on the back of Bless's neck. The words of the prophecy. What did Ginger know of the prophecy?

"Maybe you've had enough to drink," Rick said.

"Maybe you'd live a much longer and healthier life minding your own goddamn business."

Bless's head snapped up in alarm. Ginger's voice had roughened and deepened. There was a momentary flash of yellow in her eyes. Oh *heck*. Bless dared not add to any negativity by even thinking words with weighty negative connotation, but *heck* did not serve this situation well. The demon was manifesting here and now, and it wasn't good at all.

"Yes, I'm sure Rick is aware that he would live a much longer and healthier life if he let you have your strawberry daiquiris. As many as you want. Why not try the peach too? I hear it's a specialty of the house. He's picking up the tab, so knock yourself out. Will you excuse us for a moment?"

The waiter slid the strawberry daiquiri in front of Ginger and she took a sip, temporarily mollified. "Waiter, could you bring me one of the peach ones too?"

"C'mon." Bless grabbed Rick's arm and pulled him away from the table, his jaw dragging along on the floor.

She rounded the curve to the hallway where there was a bank of pay phones and rest rooms. She motioned Rick to be quiet and looked around the corner at Ginger, with her perception widened. There was the demon, still hovering over her sister, still looking pretty mellow for a demon, thank goodness.

"Jesus, what was that all about?" Rick asked. "I

thought your sister's head was going to start spinning on her shoulders for a moment."

"I advise you not to mention the good Lord's name unless you're raising your voice in prayer. And the spinning part isn't too far-fetched."

"What?" Rick said, looking confused.

"Never mind, I should have sat down and talked to you about Ginger sooner. I had to bring her with us because she has mental issues. Delusions. She can't be left alone. I'm worried sick about the baby."

Rick peeked around the corner at Ginger, chowing down on the steak the waiter had just placed in front of her. "You're right. You should have talked to me about this. This is more than you should try to be handling alone."

"Tell me about it," Bless muttered. She took a breath. "Rick, I meant to talk to you about this sooner, before we came, but I didn't get around to it. We need to go back to her place. She's getting worse and I'm worried—"

"It's out of the question."

Bless frowned, exasperated, her nerves on edge. "Maybe you don't understand. Ginger is seriously unbalanced. It's not good for us to be in your home—"

"You're not dealing with this alone. She's carrying my brother's child. We'll get her the help she needs and we'll do what needs to be done for the child. Together."

"But, but—"

He put his fingers over her lips. "No buts. Now let's go back and finish our dinner." He walked back to the table and waited for Bless, who trailed him, feeling distraught, and trying not to wring her hands. He pulled out the chair for Bless and seated her, eyed his catfish dinner, nodded in approval, and motioned for the waiter. "I'll have a peach daiquiri," he said.

Ginger grinned at him and lifted her glass.

10

Bless was spinning among the stars and galaxies. She landed on a grassy hill, the air fragrant with flowers. A nut-brown woman sat under a willow tree a little ways away. She closed her book and stood, approaching Bless with a smile and outstretched hands.

When Bless recognized her, a tremor ran through her like an electric shock. It was Maris. But it was Maris as she barely recognized her, her features alert and intelligent, her gait confident and sure.

Maris enfolded her in an embrace and stepped back and looked at her. "I've waited for you to meet me here for a long time," she said.

"Maris—this is a dream, right? What's happening? How have you changed so?"

"This isn't really a dream, more like a different place. This is my world." Maris waved her hand and everything changed. Instead of a grassy hill, they stood in a golden-leaved forest of white trees. "Let's walk," she said.

She took Bless's hand and walked down a well-trodden path. Bless followed her silently, watching the flight of the birds, the butterflies and other insects, and the scampering squirrels. It was a busy world, full of life. They entered a clearing by a bubbling brook and Maris bade her to sit. Bless gasped as she saw a white golden-horned horse, a mythical unicorn, dip its head and drink from the other side of the brook.

"Beautiful animal, isn't it?"

"Where are we?"

"The enchanted forest. I find it a nice place for a chat."

"This is where you live?" Bless said, as much a statement as a question. It made sense, Maris living in her head, in such a beatific world. No wonder she seemed so happy.

"I live in this world. There are a lot of places; this is only one of them."

"Out of all of us sisters, you didn't do so badly. I wonder why you're referred to as the one with 'nothing.' "

Maris shrugged. "Because in your world, it appears that I have nothing. My gifts aren't discernible."

"Is Miriam here too?" Bless asked.

"Yes, she is. But not exactly *here*. You realize that Miriam and I are the same person in a sense?"

"I don't understand."

"We share the same souls. We are simply different probabilities. Spawn of the multiverse and all that."

Bless still didn't understand, but she thought of Aunt Praise. She loved her dearly, but often Praise worked her last nerve. So was Maris saying that

Bless and Praise were the same person also? Bless wasn't sure she wanted to understand the physics of the soul if that were the case.

"We don't have much time," Maris said.

"Time for what?"

"Time for your training." She looked sober. "Soon you'll have to fight. And if you don't want to die, you'll have to win."

Bless was closed in on all sides by darkness. Evil menaced. She started to run, and . . . the first one struck. She eluded it with a forward flip and midair twist and exploded it from its center with a flashy burst of blue-white light that flared and caught the one next to it, and it flamed out also with a scream.

She had no time to feel triumphant because a searing pain lashed across her back. She wheeled and did a double back flip and landed on the back of the demon, grabbed his raised whip, and knocked it upside the head. She then executed a perfect triple forward axle rounder and snapped off the head of the monster with the whip, knocking the next one over with its head as if it were a bowling pin. She leaped into the heavens and swung the whip in great arcs. Legion howled in defeat—

"Wake up, wake up! Bless!" She opened her eyes to see Rick sitting on her bed grasping her shoulders in both hands.

"Thank goodness, you're finally awake. You must have been having the mother of all nightmares. You were screaming."

"Screaming?"

"Yes, and look at you, you're soaked with sweat. Let me get you a towel."

"I hate to ask, but I'm not feeling well. Do you mind getting me some ice water, please?" Bless asked.

Rick patted her hand and left for the kitchen. Bless let out a groan. She felt as if she'd run a marathon. She didn't know if she could move if she tried. Every muscle in her body ached. That must have been a nightmare he woke her from, but what preceded it certainly wasn't.

She'd undergone the mother of all battle training. It was as if she'd spent weeks with Maris, along with others, learning the techniques of hand-to-claw demon fighting. If Rick had heard her screaming, it probably was a war cry.

Bless was still scared, but she felt much more prepared and confident after her demon battle boot camp in paradise. If she had to, she'd open a can of demon whup-ass. She flexed her bicep, feeling strong and warrior-like—yeah, demons, bring it on. Then she moved her shoulder the wrong way and pain shot all the way down to her buttocks.

Maybe not quite yet, Bless thought, easing her way out of the bed, limping to the bathroom to get the ibuprofen out of the medicine cabinet. She really should lighten up on those moves a bit during demon battle. Just because she could do the cool gymnastic moves didn't necessarily mean that she should, she decided as she stifled another moan.

Bless returned to bed a moment before Rick came in bearing a luscious-looking pitcher of ice water, a tall glass, and a straw. "You seem like you're losing a lot of fluids." He touched her forehead. "You probably broke a fever during the night. It could be the flu," he murmured.

She wanted to deny it, but couldn't think of any other reason that made the slightest sense for her obvious physical distress. Rick could see by now she wasn't the workout type.

"You're not hot now," he added, caressing her face.

Oh, but she was. He brushed his lips against hers and the pain faded as she circled her arms around his neck. She was on fire. The kiss deepened, his lips firm, controlled. She ran her fingers down the muscles of his back and craved his weight on her. His solid hardness pressing, enveloping her, holding her . . . she wanted that so bad.

His tongue plundered her mouth and he moaned. "You're not feeling well," he whispered into her ear and started pulling away.

It was like somebody yanking away her blanket in subzero temperatures. No, don't go. She pulled him down upon her. "You're making me feel so . . ." At the moment his hard frame connected with her aching tissues. She gasped. "Sore," she finished, her eyes watering from the pain.

Rick rolled away immediately and stood at the side of the bed. "That's it; I'm getting you something to take for the pain."

"I took something already." She struggled to sit up in bed and Rick helped her up, fluffing pillows behind her back.

"Can I make you some tea?"

"No, the water is enough. You've been great. But you better go back to bed," Bless said, glancing at the clock, which read four in the morning. "You have to go to work."

Rick stood over her frowning. "Are you sure you're all right? This came on so quickly."

She waved him away, and picked up a glass of water. "I'll be fine, once I get back to sleep."

She drank half the glass in one draft and fell

back on the pillows. "Could you turn out the light on your way out?"

"All right." She heard his soft footsteps and then felt a kiss like a butterfly wing on her forehead. The room went dark. "Sweet dreams," he whispered.

Bless grimaced in the dark. That was one thing she didn't want to have, because as tied up inside as she was right now with desire, all her dreams would surely be about him. And now that she could have Rick in the flesh, her flesh was too sore to take it. Not fair. But to be honest, Bless was worried about way more than a missed opportunity for heavy breathing with Rick.

In that other place, Maris told her that her developmentally disabled brain was merely a flawed image of her real mind, her physical body a shadow of her real body. Maris had been very clear about the fact that your physical body dies if your etheric body is harmed or changed (Maris said nothing was truly destroyed).

Bless shifted her aching body to lie on her side. The proof of the truth of Maris's words was the pain within her body. Exertion in her etheric body reflected profoundly in her physical body. It made sense, because what Bless healed was the aura or halo-like image of a person's physical body and the flesh healed also.

Maris blithely told her not to worry; death was nothing but a change of location. Bless had looked at her like she was crazy. Maris then helpfully said Bless needed to work at wrapping her mind around the concept. That Maris was a hoot, all right. Since her sister didn't really live within her body, she didn't have that down-home attachment to her skin that Bless shared with most fully conscious folk. Maris acted as if she didn't understand the extreme unpleasantness of the whole death thing.

Bless squinted into the darkness of the room, trying to envision some worse scenarios, but the image of her dead body about topped out her imagination.

11

Bless opened her eyes. The light in her room was odd. Was this a dream-vision? She turned her head on the pillow, and felt a twinge of muscle pain that was all too real to be visionary. Her flesh felt heavy, the bed too solid. Almost disappointed to have to face the reality of the day, she focused her eyes on the dial of her clock.

"Eeek!" she exclaimed as she tried to sit up too quickly, and pain registered along with disbelief over how long she'd slept. It was almost noon! Where was Ginger?

Rick stuck his head in. "Good, you're awake in time for lunch. Wait until you taste what I cooked."

"Aren't you supposed to be at work?"

"I took a day off." Rick opened her bedroom door wide. "Smell the aroma?"

Bless smiled in spite of her worry. He looked so pleased with himself. "It smells good. What did you cook?"

"My specialty, spaghetti and meatballs. The garlic bread is in the oven, can't let it burn. I'll bring you a plate."

He headed back toward the kitchen.

Bless sat on the side of the bed and eased her feet into her house shoes. She braced herself and stood. The room whirled for a moment. She needed to find Ginger and make sure the baby was all right. The bright side was that the demon still seemed to be on the down low.

She struggled into her robe and made her way toward the sound of the television in front of the blue recliner in the den. There Ginger was perched like a brown Buddha, eyes fixed on the tube.

"Good morning," Bless said.

"More like good afternoon, you mean," Ginger replied, not taking her eyes off the screen.

Relieved that the status quo held, Bless went into the kitchen. Rick was standing in front of the stove, stirring what had to be two gallons of spaghetti sauce. She peeked into the trash and saw discarded glass jars. Spaghetti, the bachelor's specialty. A bottle of red wine, a jar of spaghetti sauce, some ground beef, store-bought garlic bread in the oven, and a salad bar salad made an easy woman-pleasin' meal.

Not that she personally knew that much about man-made woman-pleasing meals. Attention from a man like Rick was something new to her.

He stood too close, causing a tingle to curl in her lower belly. He hadn't shaved. His jaw was covered with sexy stubble. There should be a law against a man looking so delicious right when you first woke up. Made you want to go right back to bed.

"You're out of bed. How are you feeling?" he asked.

"I feel fine, and lunch smells good."

"Here, sit down, it's about ready," he said as he pulled out a chair. Then he cast a worried look toward the den. "Let me take Ginger a tray."

"Good idea. How was she doing this morning?" Bless tried not to sound apprehensive.

"In front of the television as always. I fed her breakfast. If somebody didn't feed that woman, would she starve?" Rick asked.

Bless didn't bother to answer because it was obviously a rhetorical question. Ginger wasn't about to allow herself to starve, although she was looking pretty rough lately.

Bless contemplated the physical deterioration taking place in her sister. It was the demon influence manifesting. Ginger's skin and features looked coarser, her red hair was wilder, her breath smelled fouler, and her teeth had a gray color. There was a tinge of yellow to her eyes that wasn't fading away.

If Ginger's head started spinning, if she started floating in the air and spewing pea green puke, well, it would be difficult to explain to Rick.

She'd think Ginger, so vain about her looks, would have a fit if she took a gander in a mirror and would waste no time trying to send the demon back to hell whence it came. The girl was obviously not herself.

Bless sighed. But for evil to take hold, there must be a gateway. Ginger had allowed evil into her heart by her own free will and intention. She wouldn't realize the cosmetic effect until it was far too late.

And in case that full-out demon battle commenced, Bless didn't want Rick in the house. The demon couldn't attack him physically, but it sure could cause a heavy object to drop on him or a knife to rip him open. It would cause him to doubt his sanity and would certainly scare the hell into him, so to speak.

The smart thing to do when you see an image of a demon or some demon manifestation is to scream and haul ass. Rick was a bright man. But it was his house and he was the type to think that he needed to take a stand and protect the womenfolk or some such foolishness.

Worrying about protecting Rick . . . it was eating her up. She had to get Ginger and that damn demon out of here.

"Why the long face?" Rick asked.

Bless hesitated and answered with half the truth. "Ginger isn't looking very well."

"When is her next appointment with her ob-gyn scheduled?"

Bless didn't want to tell him that not only was there no appointment, there was no doctor. The only reason she was counting on getting Ginger to a hospital to deliver would be out of pure self-interest when labor started. Ginger had never done well with pain, and Bless planned on letting her know about the joys of an epidural once hard labor hit.

"I'm starving. That looks delicious," she said, wanting to change the subject.

"I'll fix your plate. When is your sister's due date? I don't think either one of you told me."

Because we don't exactly know.

"She's going on nine months now."

"That soon? Little Malik Junior will be making an appearance any minute now."

"Her name is Glory." Bless wanted to slap her

hands over her mouth as soon as the words slipped out, but Rick only looked at her funny. He put a huge plate of spaghetti with two fist-sized meatballs in front of her. "Enjoy," he said.

The doorbell rang. "That must be my sister," Rick said.

Bless's fork froze halfway to her mouth. "Your sister is coming here?"

"She wants me to baby-sit. My mom has a doctor's appointment, and she was going to put her in a day care, but when I said I'd be home . . . besides, she's been dying to meet you all."

He was almost out of the kitchen when he paused. "Oh, she and Mom don't know the whole situation about Malik. She thinks he's taken off on one of his schemes. They are naturally worried sick. But they don't know anything about the money being gone."

Then he was out of the kitchen. Bless hurried back to her room to dress. It wouldn't do to meet a member of Rick's family for the first time, still wearing her bathrobe after twelve noon.

Bless emerged from the bedroom around ten minutes later. Rick was in the kitchen serving spaghetti to a pretty toddler around two years old with light honey skin and masses of black curly hair.

"Valerie couldn't stay. She dropped off little Valentine here and said she'd see you later when she picks her up."

Bless felt a touch of ice at her spine and turned to see Ginger padding into the kitchen.

"What's this?" Ginger asked.

"My niece Valentine."

Valentine decided it was much more fun to wear

the spaghetti than to eat it and was busy sticking gobs of tomato sauce–covered pasta in her hair. "My sister is going to kill me. Look at this child," Rick said.

"I'll bathe her," Ginger said, picking up the child. "It'll be good practice."

"Bye, bye," Valentine called, waving.

Bless started out after them.

"Bless, hold up, I want to talk to you," Rick said.

"In a moment," Bless said, "Let me go and help Ginger with——"

"She can manage to bathe one little kid herself. I've wanted to get you alone to tell you about something that happened." He hesitated. "With you and Ginger only just getting settled in here, I haven't wanted to bother you with strange goings-on . . ."

Bless's eyebrows shot up. Strange goings-on, indeed. That could be an understatement. She swallowed hard.

"Like—like what?"

"I think Swank knows Ginger is gone. My men spotted him and his boys inside Ginger's place. By the time we got in, they'd taken off. The place was trashed." He paused, looking sober. "I'm sorry. I'm waiting for the right moment to break it to Ginger."

Bless had to catch hold of the back of a chair to stop her knees from wobbling with relief. Thank goodness Rick's strange goings-on were of the human variety.

"I'll tell her. Don't worry too much about it. I know she has renter's insurance and loves to shop——"

Suddenly Bless gasped. Fear hit her as if she'd slammed into a glass wall.

"What's wrong?" Rick asked, alarmed.

"I have to go to the bathroom," she managed to get out as she took off running upstairs.

The bathroom door was locked. Bless kicked it open. Ginger was holding the little girl under the water. Bless grabbed Ginger by the hair and dragged her away, slamming her sister against the wall. Ginger sagged down over the toilet.

Bless lifted Valentine out of the bathtub. The girl was still and unbreathing, but life remained. Energies swirled around Bless, and she poured healing energies into the child.

She heard a roar as blackness darted toward her to reclaim the child. Bless snarled and slapped it away with the power as she would a gnat.

Valentine coughed and spewed out water from her lungs as she gasped in life-giving air. Her honey skin regained its rosy undertone. The toddler started screaming and sobbing as Bless carried her downstairs and ran straight into Rick. He peered up at the open bathroom with the mess and Ginger still lying in a heap by the toilet, giggling.

"What the hell happened here?" Rick demanded.

Bless continued down the stairs with Valentine, not wanting to tell Rick that he had gotten it exactly right. Hell happened, and she'd been just in the nick of time to stop it.

"Valentine had a mishap in the bathtub," she answered.

"Fully dressed? Your sister was bathing my niece fully dressed?"

Ginger hadn't bothered to take off Valentine's shoes before trying to drown her. Bless felt tears sting her eyes as she thought of what might have happened. She was going to have to confide in Rick. It was past time to act. Ginger was becoming too dangerous. She had to get Rick to help her get Ginger back to Red Creek somehow.

12

Bless took off Valentine's clothes, put an old T-shirt on her, and tenderly tucked her into bed. She soothed Valentine to sleep with the power and flooded the room with white light while she widened her perceptions. If a demon was coming, she needed to see it. But there was nothing. She sensed no familiar tarry demon miasma.

Rick leaned against the doorway, watching her. "You're good with kids," he said.

"It's the nursing touch."

"No, it's more than that. You're the natural motherly type."

"Matronly?" Bless said, her voice teasing and gentle.

"No. Womanly in a sexy, earth-mother sort of way."

The man was going to cause her to fall over and faint if he kept saying things like that.

"Come, I need to talk to you," he said.

She went the little ways into the living room, not

wanting to be too far from Valentine. She kept her perceptions open.

"For two people who live together, we seem to get to spend a very small amount of time together before we're inevitably interrupted," Rick said.

"It does seem that way. But I need to talk to you too, about something serious. About Ginger."

The expression on Rick's face said, Yeah, I wondered when you were going to finally get around to this.

"Have you been able to tell that she's getting worse?"

"I'm not stupid, Bless. Ginger seems unstable at best."

Bless drew in a breath. "You could say that. I think she's too much for me to handle here. I want to get her back home, back to Red Creek."

"It makes sense except for one thing."

"What's that?

"Swank."

"I'm not that worried about Swank."

"You should be. You may not notice it, but you are under my protection, such as it is. In Red Creek, I couldn't protect Ginger. If he got wind where she was—"

"There is far more to worry about than Swank. Aunt Praise can put up a warding spell and that will take care of him, but—"

"A what kind of spell? You're joking. These guys deal with guns, not spells."

Bless bit her lip, and studied her shoes. "There's more in this world than meets the eye. And there is way more to worry about than some small-time gangster."

"Like what?"

"Like demons."

Silence. Bless peeked at Rick and wanted to cringe. He was staring at her like she'd lost her last marble. What could she say?

"Did you ever see *The Exorcist*?" she asked.

Rick sighed. "And here I thought you were the sensible one."

"You need to hear me out. Ginger tried to kill Valentine. She's under demon influence."

"Jesus."

"Praying isn't a bad idea, but I'd advise you to do it with considerably more feeling."

She was losing Rick. He was about ready to have them both carted off to the funny farm.

Maybe it was time. There was a dread feeling in the house, something new, something worse. It was emanating from upstairs. "Let's find Ginger."

She stood and held out a hand to Rick. He looked at her. "All I'm asking you to do is to suspend your disbelief for a few moments. Follow me and discern what your own eyes tell you."

He stood. "*The Exorcist*, huh? And you want me to go up the stairs? Don't you realize this isn't a black thing? If there's a demon in the house, the direction we're supposed to go is out the door," he said, pointing, not quite able to suppress his grin.

So he was able to joke about it. That was a good sign. Bless's mouth was dry and she swallowed hard. She called silently upon the guardians to protect Valentine, and she motioned Rick to follow her as she made her way up the stairs.

She felt it emanate from Rick's room. Black and cold. She touched the door and shuddered, reverberations of demon laughter ringing through her body. She glanced at Rick. Apparently he heard nothing. He was frowning, she guessed at the thought of Ginger being in his room without permission. The doorknob was like ice.

She reached out and turned it.

Ginger was exactly in the middle of Rick's bed, buck-naked. The room was twenty degrees colder than the hall and they exhaled steamy puffs of air.

"What the hell?" Rick said.

Bless really wished he wouldn't say that. The demon was coiled over Ginger, overlying her aura with its foulness. Rick couldn't perceive the demon, which existed mostly in the other plane.

"Get off my bed and put some clothes on," Rick ordered.

Ginger hissed and a babble of some strange language poured out of her mouth. Her eyes were definitely glowing yellow.

Rick stepped back a step. "I don't think it's an exorcist your sister needs; I think it's a shrink."

Then she started to levitate off the bed, hanging in midair, and Rick's skin took on an interesting gray tone.

"Um, Rick, why don't you take Valentine and see about that door you mentioned. I have the skills to handle it from here."

To his credit and her dismay, he didn't bolt right away. "Are you sure you're going to be all right?"

The demon uncoiled. It was preparing to strike her. "Go, Rick!" she screamed.

Bless had no time to see if Rick was hauling tail because she slipped into the other place and grasped blue energy to counter the yellow-black fire the demon issued forth. The demon roared, shaking the house to its foundations. Bless raised her arms. It was on.

She soared into the air and poised over it matrix-style. The demon was surprised.

So, it thought it could toy with her for a while, did it? Demons loved to toy. Po' demon, toy with this. She kicked it in the head. Then she flipped to the other side of the room, gathering her energies for the kill.

Pissed off, it grew larger, its mouth opening as if to engulf her.

She crouched, waiting. Waited until it came closer. Closer. The air grew slimy with the demon's fetid breath. It extended a fang to eviscerate her slowly. She exploded power upward through its essence with white energy, breaking the bonds that held it together.

It screamed as it shattered and dissolved into nothing but a funky residue of black goo.

Bless snapped back to herself and opened her eyes to see Ginger sitting on the side of the bed and wrapping herself in a blanket. "It's gone. It's gone, isn't it, Bless?" she asked, a tremor in her voice.

Bless nodded.

"Thank goodness. That thing was out of control." She jumped off the bed and stared at her face in a mirror. "Look at me! I must have gained thirty pounds! I look like hell."

Bless exhaled. It seemed that her sister was back to her old self.

Rick burst through the door brandishing a cross, a Star of David, a garlic clove, and a .45 magnum.

He about tripped over his own feet when he saw the two sisters standing in the middle of his bedroom. Ginger was still frowning at her reflection in the mirror. He squinted at Ginger. "Are you all right?"

How could Bless **not** love this man? She didn't want to tell him that neither the garlic nor the .45 would work on demons, and the religious symbols were iffy at best. "Was the Star of David a backup in case the cross didn't work or vice versa?" she asked.

He looked sheepish. "I left Valentine with a cop, because I couldn't leave you here to face . . . whatever you were dealing with alone."

Bless did what she'd been wanting to do for these past days and walked into the haven of Rick's strong arms. "The demon is gone," she said.

"It's not like you deserve a medal. It could be back," Ginger said.

"It won't be back," Bless said.

"I hope not. Where are my clothes?" Ginger exited to return to her room.

Bless leaned against Rick. His arms were strong and warm around her. He was finally here to hold her up and share her burden. She'd felt so alone. A sob welled up from deep within. It had been so long.

He gathered her closer, and kissed her tears dry. "I'm here now, baby. I'm here."

13

"Let's get out of here. The Princess Royale Hotel has an excellent revolving restaurant at the top. Then . . ." Rick let his words trail away, his lips buried in her hair.

Bless understood exactly what he was saying. Then after they ate, they would get a room. Her dreams would finally come true.

She lifted her head and gently touched her mouth to his in answer. They stood together in silence. His hands moved over the curves of her hips and rested on her lower back. "It's never been quite like this with any woman before. It's as if I know you," Rick whispered against her ear.

"Yes," Bless breathed. At last, he felt it too. There was a mystery that connected them, a cord between their hearts. She didn't understand what it meant, or what exactly his role or purpose was beyond the fact that, somehow, he was a part of her, as necessary as her flesh.

"Meant to be." Rick's words were more a benediction than a prayer, a pronouncement of what was. He pulled her to him and caught her mouth in a kiss.

Bless melted. His scent, his touch, his hungry kiss spun her every sense out of control. She felt herself opening like a rose blossom for him. This was her need, her desire, the aching emptiness that all her life she never could come close to filling.

In an instant, Rick's kiss overflowed her soul and filled her with . . . was this love? This innate acceptance and recognition of this man with all his flaws, and all his human failings? Somehow she knew the depths and heights of his spirit and loved it wholly. She knew he felt the same way about her. Meant to be? Yes. A woman is meant to love and be loved.

Life after life, the circle turns.

Bless stiffened. "What's wrong?" Rick asked.

She didn't want to tell him that she was hearing voices. With Ginger off the deep end, it seemed too much like an excess of mental imbalance in the family. She felt as if she were on a crazy carnival ride that was on the verge of veering out of control. She'd save the revelations of the voices she heard and visions she saw for later.

"I need to get Valentine," he said. "I'll be back in a few minutes." He dropped a kiss on her forehead before hurrying out of the room.

The carnival ride tilted and went around the bend. She'd been going through too much compressed into too short a space of time. Voices and visions, invisible demon battles, family legends and a vague prophecy with the dire watermarking of Armageddon on it, small-time gangsters, a disappearing babydaddy, and maybe having to save the world in addition to saving her infant niece from her murderous mama. A dark stranger in dreams materializing in the flesh to hold her and proffer soft kisses and tender touches to make her burn and yearn and desire like she'd never imagined possible.

Way too much. Bless sank to the edge of Rick's bed and rocked back and forth—a soothing motion that she'd often seen Maris do. And the worst thing was, Bless had the feeling that it all had only begun.

A ring of the doorbell, insistent and shrill, cut through her thoughts. The bell rang again. Why couldn't Ginger get it? she wondered.

Bless hurried to answer the door bell and pulled open the door to see an attractive, slim woman with beautiful Hershey silken skin and shoulder-length braids standing there. "Hello, you must be one of Malik's friends that Rick has staying here. He told us all about you. Hi, I'm Valerie, Rick's sister."

Bless stood aside from the door to allow the woman entry. "Rick and Valentine will be back in a moment. Won't you come in and have a seat."

Valerie studied Bless's stomach. "Rick said you were almost due? You are carrying the baby well, I must say."

Bless cocked her head and looked at the woman. She knew she was a little plump, but damn, she knew her stomach wasn't that big. "You're thinking about my sister. Ginger is in her room; she must be resting," Bless said.

Valerie had the grace to appear embarrassed. "I'm sorry. I have a mouth that outruns my brain and is big enough to hold one foot or the other."

Bless smiled. "You had me ready to make an appointment for the next Weight Watchers meeting, but that's not necessarily a bad thing."

"You're not that fat. Big bones run in our family. Either we're heavy from childhood or, like me, one of those who can eat everything and burn it off. It lasts until we hit forty-five and then our rear ends blow up to the size of beach balls."

Bless laughed. "Curves aren't a bad thing as long as the beach balls don't tip you backwards."

"I wouldn't mind having some curves in the right places. My husband says he can't wait until I get older and develop some junk in my trunk. It's always something," Valerie said, with a sigh.

The front door opened and Valentine ran in with Rick following behind her. "Mama!" she called.

Valerie picked her up and swung her in her arms. "Thanks, Rick, I owe you one."

"You owe me more than one, woman," he said.

"I have to run and get supper on," Valerie said. "It was nice meeting you . . ."

"Bless," she offered her name.

"Bless, unusual name. I like it. Maybe next time I come by, I'll meet Ginger."

"Where is Ginger?" Rick asked.

"I think she's sleeping," Bless said. But something didn't feel right. It was too quiet. The atmosphere was heavy and sodden.

Valerie picked up her daughter and carried her out the door. Bless's uneasiness increased. "I'm going to go and check on Ginger."

"I'll call the Royale for reservations," Rick said.

Bless tapped on the closed door of Ginger's room. "Go away, Bless. I'm sick," she heard Ginger say in a faint voice.

Bless pushed open Ginger's bedroom door and the sour smell of bile assaulted her nostrils. Ginger was curled up on the bed in a fetal position, moaning softly.

"What's wrong, sis?" she asked.

"I've been puking my guts out. My head and stomach are killing me."

Bless touched Ginger, no fever. She picked up her wrist to feel the ropes of her veins and arteries. There was no red, violet pounding of stretched tissues due to high pressure.

"The flu?"

"I don't think so." Ginger moaned. "My stomach."

Bless extended her open palm over her sister's stomach. Glory was fine, but there was something awry.

She sensed streaks of brown-black radiating from Ginger's upper right abdomen throughout her body, spreading malaise. Poisons were building.

Ginger's liver was malfunctioning. An alarm went off in Bless's head. They had to get Ginger to the hospital now. Glory had to come out. Bless touched Glory. She'd be all right if they delivered her. But could it happen in time?

Bless raced from the room calling for Rick. "Pull up the car; we have to get Ginger to the hospital."

"Which one?"

"The closest one. She has got to have the baby now."

As soon as Rick pulled into the ER drive, Bless hopped out of the car and got a wheelchair from the ER entrance. Rick lifted Ginger into it, then Bless took off for the sliding doors at a run.

"Please, I have an emergency here!"

Ginger was on a stretcher in record time.

"What seems to be the problem?" the doctor asked.

"She is going into crisis. She is in pain, right upper abdominal quadrant with severe nausea and vomiting, sudden onset. It's not preeclampsia—"

"Preeclampsia?" the doctor said, cutting her words off and taking out a clipboard. "Does she have a history? Who's her OB?"

"Ma'am, we need you to give us her insurance card and sign some papers," the clerk said, grabbing Bless's arm.

"You don't understand, this is an emergency. The baby needs to be delivered one way or the other now!"

Several nurses had already got Ginger on a cart, hooking her up to a fetal monitor, while another quickly slipped a Foley catheter between her legs.

"Ma'am, you need to come with me now! We need the patient's insurance information," the clerk insisted in a shrill voice.

"She doesn't have any health insurance."

The doctor, clerk, and Bless swore the entire ER staff stilled and turned to stare with the same horror as if Bless had sprouted tentacles and announced they'd arrived from Mars.

A nurse approached and spoke to the resident in a low tone Bless couldn't overhear. "Her blood pressure is normal? No protein in her urine? Thanks," the doctor said to a nurse, continuing to ignore Bless.

"No insurance? Why didn't you take her to Slater?" the clerk said with an intake of breath.

"I'm not taking her to the city hospital. She's here and you have to treat her, it's the law," Bless snapped.

"Not if it's not an emergency, we don't," the resident said.

"She'll get Medicaid," Bless hissed.

The clerk recoiled as if Bless had pronounced that her sister would get leprosy. "This is a private hospital," she sniffed.

"Your sister isn't in labor," the doctor told Bless. "Her vital signs and urine are normal. The baby is doing fine according to the fetal monitor. If you want some sort of treatment for her, you'll have to take her elsewhere." He wrote a note on her clipboard. "She's discharged. The nurse will give you instructions. You need to go to her OB for follow-up first thing in the morning—"

"Help me get Ginger back in the car," Bless called out to Rick, who was walking in.

"But I just parked," he said, puzzled.

"Unpark then, and quickly. We have to roll. I'm going to get Ginger."

Bless slapped the nurse's hand away and removed the catheter herself.

"Ginger, get up. We have to get you to another hospital."

"Why? I feel terrible. I'm scared, Bless."

"By the time these folk deigned to figure out your diagnosis and treat you, it might be too late . . . the best thing is to get to another hospital."

She let Ginger lean on her heavily and helped her to the entrance. Bless's mind was too unfocused to gather the energies needed for healing. She'd made it out the door when Rick pulled up. She helped Ginger into the front seat and got behind her.

"Roll to Slater, Rick, and don't waste time."

Ginger was heaving into a plastic bag. Bless felt something give inside Ginger and almost panicked. She closed her eyes and gathered herself, concentrating, pulling elemental energies from the earth, the original mother. She reached over the seat and touched Ginger's shoulder, pouring healing energies, balancing and holding.

Ginger was starting to bleed. It was taking all Bless had to stabilize her sister's body now. If she went now, so would Glory.

When they pulled up to Slater, Bless whispered to Rick, "Go and get somebody. They need to bring a cart. She's worse."

Her sister was mumbling, lapsing into a semiconscious state between worlds.

A few seconds letter, someone in scrubs came running to the car. "What's the problem?"

"HELLP, I believe. She just lost consciousness."

They got Ginger out of the car and on the cart in five seconds flat.

"What did you say was the problem?" the resident asked.

"HELLP. That's Hemolysis, Elevated Liver Enzymes and Low PLatelet Syndrome," Bless shouted. The resident nodded in quick understanding and touched the area of her liver and shook her head. "Page Strauss stat. Put her in OR eight and prep her for an emergency C-section."

A nurse approached Bless. "The admissions desk is this way."

"I need to be with my sister. I'd like to observe the procedure. I'm an emergency room registered nurse and I'll stay out of the way."

They had to allow her to stay with her sister. Her

presence might mean the difference between Ginger's and Glory's life and death.

Relief streamed through Bless when the nurse said, "I'll show you where the surgical dressing area is."

14

Bless dressed in scrubs and made her way to the metal sinks outside the OR. She washed her hands carefully even though she knew it wasn't necessary. The motions were soothing and distracted her from her worry. She watched her sister getting a spinal block through the glass window. She studied the fetal monitor readout. Glory was still doing all right.

Bless constricted her perceptions. This hospital was nothing like the one at home. She couldn't imagine working a twelve hour shift here, fully sensitive to the energies swirling around her. The pain, the death, the despair, the number of confused entities, mixed with triumph, healing, humanity, grace, and release.

There was so much in this one place, so many beginnings and endings.

A nurse went into the OR with two units of blood. A second nurse picked up Ginger's arm and listened carefully while the nurse read the label on the blood, matching it to what Ginger's identification bracelet said. They both signed a form.

Bless bit her lip, put her mask in place, and entered the room. Ginger was slipping, leaking her life. She needed that blood.

"I'm Bless Sanderson, an RN from Red Creek," Bless said. "They said it was all right to observe." She stood to the right of the anesthesiologist, who was checking the monitors and notating Ginger's vital signs. She could touch Ginger's head.

The surgical assistant and circulating nurse barely acknowledged her; they were busy opening packs and setting up shiny instruments, and counting gauze and needles on blue cloth–draped tables.

Two doctors entered and took their place at Ginger's nether regions.

"Hello, Ginger, I'm Dr. Strauss, and we're going to deliver this baby for you," one said cheerily.

Since Ginger was barely conscious, she didn't respond at all.

Rick hated hospitals. He hated the smell, the atmosphere, the tension, and he hated the waiting most of all. He hated this place particularly. It was the city's Level 1 trauma center.

How many times had he sat here in this room and waited to hear if somebody had pulled through their surgery for gunshot wounds?

He sat in the surgical waiting room chair fighting the feeling of déjà vu. Seven years ago, waiting with his mother, his brother, and his sister when Dad was shot. *Would he be all right?* Of course he would. He had to.

When the doctor came out, with one look at his

face, they all knew that Daddy wasn't all right. Mom refused to move, so it was up to him, the oldest, to approach the doctor and hear the news. To not shake or waver or allow the tears to run down his own cheeks. And then try to tell his mother.

She turned her head when he approached. When he started to speak, she got up and walked away. Her heels clicked down the hall as he heard her sobs recede in the distance.

God, he hated this place.

He sensed he was being stared at and lifted his head. He looked straight into the eyes of Swank. Great. This was all he needed. He nodded, acknowledging the man. Swank was sitting with a small group of men. He got up and moved by Rick. "Mint?" he offered.

"No thanks."

"One of your men shot?" Swank asked.

"No, I'm here because of a friend."

"One of my boys was taken down. Stupid wannabe. Made no sense." Swank sighed. "I been wanting to talk to you about your brother. Been putting it off, man."

"What is it?"

Swank sighed again, real heavy. "We found him. He wasn't hiding and he doesn't have the money." He studied his shoes. "He was dead, man. We didn't do it."

"You're lying."

Swank didn't say anything and Rick felt sick. He never wanted to consider that Malik could be dead. He thought the worst was that he took off with the money and Rick was going to have to figure out how to break it to Mama that her youngest was on the lam. But he knew Mama would be all right as long as she knew her baby was all right.

But this. No. Tears stung Rick's eyes and he stood and walked to the men's room. He splashed cold water on his face. Not enough. He slammed his hand against the hard tile, the pain radiating down his arm. Leaning on his forehead, he breathed in gulps of air.

Moments passed. Men came and went, respecting his pain. He got a paper towel, wiped his face, and returned to the waiting room.

Swank was sitting in the same place, still studying his feet. "Where is he?" Rick asked.

"Brushyclean Creek way up by Sugar Hill off the highway."

"I know the place."

"The bitch did it. She took the money, framed your brother, and offed him."

"How do you know?"

"Who else? And she wasn't subtle about it. Stuck one of her own kitchen knives in him. Wrapped him up in her shower curtain and drove him up north and dumped him in the creek. Go get the fucking evidence," Swank said.

Rick rubbed his throbbing head before pulling out his cell phone.

Swank stood. "You always been fair with us, Jensen. It's a damned shame about what that bitch did to your brother."

Rick raised an eyebrow. Swank was swimming in temporary solidarity although, if he'd found Malik with his money, he would have killed him right after saying hello.

He had to take one thing at a time. The first was to find out if what Swank was telling him was true.

"Let me handle my own business," Rick said.

Swank nodded. "What about my money?"

"Give me until tomorrow morning. Call me."

"All right." Swank stood. "I'm sorry about your brother, man," he said, and he returned to his seat.

Forensics strung yellow tape around the creek. Rick sat in his car and stared into the night, unseeing, unthinking, and trying not to feel. His partner got in the passenger seat. Wendell Wright seemed like Rick's opposite on surface glance—he was white, middle-aged, paunchy, and balding, a family man. But in personality, they were similar, and over the years, they'd grown close.

"Get me a cigarette," Rick said. He'd quit smoking with great effort two years ago, but now he couldn't think of anything he needed more except his brother back alive.

"No," Wendell said. "I'll go with you," his partner added, touching his shoulder.

Rick got a tissue out of his pocket and blew his nose. "Thanks," he said, and started his car to go and tell his mother another thing she couldn't bear to hear. "Could you call Valerie for me and tell her to meet me at Mom's house? I can't talk to her now."

Wendell, good friend that he was, pulled out his cell phone without a word.

"Yes, it's an emergency," Wendell said to Valerie. "He'll tell you when he gets there. Just go, all right? I don't know what you should tell her. Bye. Okay." He put away the phone. "She'll be there," he said.

"Thanks, buddy."

When Rick pulled up to his mother's house, Valerie was waiting for them. She held the door open. "What is going on?" she asked.

"Where's Mama?"

"In the kitchen."

His mother was standing over the sink, washing pots and pans. She never believed in putting them in the dishwasher. "Mama, come into the living room. I have something to tell you," Rick said.

"Hi there, Wendell. You two want something to eat? I have some brisket."

"Mama."

"All right." She wiped her hands on a dishtowel. They all followed her to the living room.

"Well, everybody, sit down," she said.

Rick sat next to his mother. "It's about Malik."

His mother looked away. He looked at Valerie and the tears had already started running down his sister's cheeks. "He's gone, Mom. We found his body."

Valerie sobbed. His mother was unmoving. "Mama?"

She thrust out a hand, her face turned away. "I buried my husband and that was hard enough. I'm not burying any of my children. I'm not doing it. I'm not doing it, hear? I'm not!" His mother's voice had risen to a scream. "I'll die first." She stood and ran toward her bedroom. Rick caught her in his arms and pulled her to him. She stiffened, and then collapsed against him.

"I can't, Rick. Don't you understand?" she whispered. It felt as if her spirit dissolved, and blew away.

"I know, Mom. I know." He captured her and held her together while their tears mingled.

Bless held her breath as Glory was pulled from Ginger's belly, covered with blood. The baby grimaced with the cold, her skin dark bluish gray.

They cleansed her and cut the cord and she wailed, pinking brown. The nurse received her and Bless moved to her.

"May I?" Bless held Glory while the nurse recorded the newborn's condition and responses. She was so beautiful. They let Bless swaddle her with blankets and put a little cap on her head. She held her to her chest. Nothing would ever happen to this baby, she vowed.

The nurse handed her a tissue and Bless looked at it, surprised, until she felt the wetness under her mask. Tears were streaming down her cheeks.

"Is the mother going to breastfeed?"

Ginger said she wasn't about to let some brat stretch out her titties.

"No, she prefers that Glory be bottle-fed."

"Ms. Sanderson, do you want to hold your baby?" the nurse asked Ginger, bending over to her ear.

Ginger turned her head away. "Take it away," she croaked.

"We're taking the patient to recovery now. Would you like to accompany her or go with the baby to the nursery?" the nurse asked.

Glory was warm against her breast. How could she let her go? "I'll go to the nursery," Bless answered. With the delivery of the baby, Ginger had immediately stabilized. She'd be fine. Bless cradled the baby and hummed a snatch of a lullaby she didn't remember learning. Glory needed her now.

15

Bless was teetering on the edge of panic and exhaustion. She was afraid to sleep, afraid that the baby would be taken to her mother unattended and Ginger would suffocate little Glory or snap her neck.

Bless sensed black currents of murder in her sister. Rick was gone, leaving only a cryptic note that he had to take care of family matters. Death was in the air tonight. Premonitions trailed like dark ribbons floating on a dread breeze. *Somebody is going to die tonight.* Whispers floated in the air.

Glory slept against her shoulder, a precious bundle. Bless studied her baby face and knew it was time to go. She'd flee with the baby. Ginger would press charges, say she kidnapped her, but Bless would stay a step ahead of her. She had savings and Aunt Praise would help. Yes, it was time.

There was an ache in her chest, a beginning of the pain to come. Although she'd barely had time to know Rick, leaving him was like ripping out her heart. Meant to be, he'd said. All she'd have left of him were her dreams.

The nurses were sitting in chairs, feeding babies, charting. The nursery was dim and quiet.

Bless stood, and went to Glory's primary nurse for the shift. "I'm going to take her to peek at her mama."

The nurse nodded and Bless walked down the hall, Glory in her arms. She passed Ginger's room and kept walking. She thought she saw a smoky shimmer out of the corner of her eye, but it wasn't enough to make her pause. She pushed the down button of the elevator and waited impatiently for the doors to open. She got in.

The elevator light flickered, dimmed. Bless's heart pounded and she gathered energies, alert. *"You thought you were going to get away with her, bitch sister of mine? Don't you get it? She lives, I die. That's an elementary equation."* It was Ginger's voice, resonant and commanding.

Bless blinked and saw Ginger, sitting straight up in her hospital bed, somehow fully recovered from her surgery. She looked fabulous, hair arranged, makeup on, her belly deflated. But that wasn't what made Bless's mouth dry in fear. Ginger was surrounded by demons. Demons guised as beautiful women. They ringed her like she was their high priestess.

Worse, Bless recognized some of the symbols that Ginger had made in the room. Black magic. Ginger had summoned the demons. Did she believe she was controlling them? Bless shuddered.

"Bring the baby back and I'll do it now," Ginger's voice thundered. Her eyes flashed red.

Bless knew what Ginger meant to do. "No," she said.

"Do it or suffer the consequences. The demons can cause you to be ripped into tiny pieces."

In answer, Bless ringed herself and Glory with blue fire. She heard something close and felt what might have been the heat of angelic swords. "You have no power here," she whispered.

There was a hiss of fury. The elevator chimed the first floor, the light normal. The door slid open and Rick stood there with another man and two cops, looking as if he were a washrag wrung dry.

"Bless, where are you going with that baby?" Rick asked.

"I just needed to stretch my legs. I was taking her for a walk down to the gift shop."

"I need to talk to you. It's serious." He took her by the arm and led her back on the elevator. The other three men didn't meet her eyes. Bless stared with a feeling of dread at the blinking lights that flashed the floors back to where she'd come from.

"Bless," Rick said.

She looked into his eyes and wondered why they held such pain. "These men are going to your sister's room," Rick said. He nodded at the policemen in uniform. "They're going to remain outside her room until she leaves the hospital. We're placing her under arrest for—for the murder of my brother."

She didn't feel surprised or alarmed at the news. Ginger apparently had layers like an onion. A rotten one beneath the outer skin.

But she flinched against the waves of pain emanating from Rick. She pulled up her reserves and touched his cheek, strengthening him, sending him peace . . . and love.

"Rick, are you getting off the elevator or what?" the white man said.

Bless brought herself to the moment and walked from the elevator, Rick following. "Let me take Glory to the nursery," she said. The baby awakened and lay gurgling against her shoulder. She needed changing.

She'd reached the nursery and handed Glory to the nurse when she heard yelling in the hallway, screams, people running, and the hoarse shouts of the policemen. The demons? It was not possible. It was always against their purposes to manifest so openly.

She ran toward the noise and smelled the death before she sensed it. Ginger's room. One of the uniformed cops was bent over heaving outside her door.

The room was covered with blood. A young man was lying in the middle of Ginger's bed. He was split open down the middle. Ginger was nowhere to be found.

Later that evening, Bless supposed she shouldn't feel content, and she felt guilty for it. But that's how it was, a warm and glowing satisfaction. She sweetly savored riding back to the haven of Rick's home with him by her side and newborn Glory strapped in an infant seat.

For the moment she put aside her dark foreboding that her respite would be as short as it was sweet.

"I don't see how Ginger could manage to kill Swank as gruesome as that, a man in his prime," Rick said.

"Ginger had help, powerful help, and plenty of it."

She saw Rick visibly shudder. "Are you meaning that demon stuff?"

"Yes, that's what I'm meaning."

Rick drove on, his brow furrowed. Bless could almost feel the mental effort he was exerting in trying to wrap his mind around the concept of demons.

"And to think I never even believed in ghosts," he murmured.

"Ghosts are usually harmless, confused souls. Demons are actively malevolent. They have never been human and carry a common hatred for humankind."

"I learned in church that they are fallen angels."

"Some have been angels; many haven't."

Rick glanced at her. "How do you know so much about demons?"

Bless paused. "I don't know," she said. It was the only truthful answer.

"Did she use demons to kill my brother?"

Bless felt the jarring upset within him. He was imagining his brother undergoing the terror and torture that Swank went through.

"I don't think so. Somehow I think I would have sensed it. I sensed darkness gathering around Ginger recently. I think the baby has been protected to an extent."

"Why does the child need to be protected?"

"Ginger's purpose is to kill her. The demons are bent towards that purpose too. I don't know who is using whom, but I suspect that they are using her. They want Glory dead."

"Why?"

"She has some part to play in the battle of Armageddon."

"Whoa. Time out. So now you're telling me we're heading toward Armageddon?"

Bless nodded. "The next generation, but we'll be alive to see it."

He said something unintelligible under his breath.

"Or die through it," she added.

Rick was silent at that.

"So demons could storm the house at any moment?" he asked finally.

"I don't think so, especially with Ginger gone. I'll cleanse every space within the walls, make it a fortress, a haven of sorts. Remember that no matter what, heavenly justice is in charge and there is always order. Chaos cannot prevail. Evil has to be invited inside."

"I never got the chance to ask you how you made like an exorcist and got rid of the demon who was hoisting Ginger up in the air?"

Bless hesitated. "I battled it."

"You what? How the hell do you battle a demon?" Rick shot a guilty look upward. "Sorry."

"He doesn't quibble so much over words; it's the heart that matters," she said, shifting in her seat. Demon battle was difficult to explain. "You can't perceive me battling a demon. Somebody on this plane, in this vibration, rarely sees a demon or any psychic phenomena."

"Why?"

"If the majority of humans believed in magic, they might put faith in something other than themselves and their science. They might believe in demons. If they believed in demons, they might believe in angels. If that happened, humans might start to truly believe in God instead of merely having a form of godly devotion. This is terrifying to demons. It would mean the destruction of demons and possibly the end of evil itself. You may never see any psychic phenomena or a demon although hanging with me it's far more likely. But in general, it doesn't suit their purposes."

"So how do you battle them?"

Bless sighed. Rick was a man who didn't lose sight of the point. "I move into where the demons dwell, a plane of lower vibration. I leave my body here. A demon can't harm my body directly, and I keep them too occupied to bother with it while I'm out. In the other place, they are physical, and I'm not. Here, it's vice versa. I concentrate the elemental energies most appropriate to the situation or demon—earth, fire, air, or water—and I break the bonds of their being."

"Oh," Rick said.

Bless stared out the window. She supposed it was a lot to absorb.

"What happens if you lose?" Rick suddenly asked.

"I die."

16

They stopped at an all-night Wal-Mart and bought a crib, blanket, sleepers, bottles, diapers, and other baby things. Rick pushed the shopping cart with the baby carrier inside. Little Glory was sleeping. Bless didn't feel déjà vu exactly; it was more like a feeling of rightness, deep-down satisfaction. *The way things were meant to be.*

She added an extra pack of newborn diapers to the cart. "That's enough," she said. "Let's go home."

The thermostat was all the way up on the drive back. Heat was building. Rick moistened his lips and glanced at her, their glances a flashpoint of desire. A familiar burning tingling started down between her legs. Oh my, it was getting hot in here.

Rick pulled into the drive and unlocked the door. They unloaded the car in a few minutes. Rick opened up the stroller that converted into a bassinet. "This will do for tonight," he said.

Rick carried it up the stairs and set it outside his bedroom door. Bless followed behind him, cradling Glory in her arms.

She settled the baby in the bassinet. Glory slept peacefully through the transfer. An easy baby.

"Bless." Rick was standing in his doorway, clad only in a pair of dark blue lounging pants. She turned to him and met his eyes. It was getting way too hot in here.

"I want you," he said.

She followed him into his room. He stood in front of her and trailed a finger down from her temple to her cheeks, tracing her lips. "It seems as if I've wanted you forever," he said.

Bless was burning up. She could only take him in, a living fantasy come true. Her eyes closed as he leaned forward and his mouth gently touched hers. He tested and tasted the contours of her lips with his, then his tongue teased her mouth gently open. He learned her mouth, taking his time with the lesson until she moaned and tried to press against him.

He cupped her breasts with his hands instead. "May I?" he asked.

She could only nod wordlessly. He unbuttoned her blouse and let it fall to the floor. He unhooked her bra with one hand and it followed.

He eased her slacks down her legs, his hands tantalizingly molding the hills of her buttocks and the fleshy mounds of her thighs. Then he slid off her panties. He stepped back and simply looked at her.

Bless felt her cheeks heat. She started to cringe, to fold and hide, but he stepped closer and grasped her shoulders, looking into her eyes. "You're beautiful," he said. "I think you're magnificent."

Bless sensed only truth and passion in his words. She trembled at the feel of his big jutting erection against her hip through the soft fabric of his pants.

All she wanted was for him to throw her on the bed and give her all of that.

It seemed as if she was going to get what she wanted because he moved her to the bed and tumbled her backward. Then his tongue licked her breasts, gently rotating around the aureoles, stiffening her nipples into hard buttons. He sucked on one breast then the other, the pulling and tugging feeling as if it was reaching right down to her feminine core. Her knees parted. She wanted, needed him inside, emptiness aching to be filled.

"Don't make me wait."

He kissed her lips and the pants disappeared. His penis sprang free, a key to her lock. He moved over her, and she arched up against him, eagerly opening.

She knit her legs around his back and felt him from the width of his shoulders, to the slim narrowness of his hips and muscular thighs. He was at her gate. She opened wide and he eased inside, the hot rings of his penis grazing her smooth walls. He filled her up and up and she couldn't help saying hallelujah because the man felt too good.

He moved and she moved with him, her walls contracting against him. It was not a dream, but meant to be.

Sweet and real hard flesh and friction building and building in the now time. Her time.

She was rising. He looked into her eyes and asked wordlessly if she was almost there.

"Yes, yes," she said.

And he plunged in deep, carrying her with him over the edge to that little death and back again.

Meant to be.

* * *

Malik's funeral was on a bright, beautiful crisp winter day. Uncharacteristically warm, the sun shined cruelly, highlighting what he was missing down in the cold, dark earth.

Bless held little Glory in her arms, Rick at her side. He supported his mother, Violet, her plump face looking drawn, weary, and swollen with tears.

Valerie stood next to Bless, with her husband and little Valentine.

Bless had felt awkward at first being included in the intimate family circle at such a tragic time. Being the sister of the suspected killer didn't help either.

Bless sat beside Violet for long hours with her new grandchild, Malik's daughter. Bless knew that no one could prepare themselves for losing a child. It was probably one of the hardest blows a soul could suffer. But Glory gurgled and cooed up at her grandmother, and the new life soothed a bit of the pain.

Rick moved forward to stand at his mother's side as she grasped a handful of dirt to throw on Malik's coffin. Bless felt a chill come over her, a premonition that alerted her that something was going to happen. There was a shimmer, and she saw the outline of a handsome young black man standing by his coffin, looking sad. Malik? Then he looked straight at her. He raised his hands, which he'd been holding against his abdomen, and they were dripping blood. Then his facial expression changed to anger and he faded away.

Bless sighed. Malik's spirit was still earthbound and that was too bad. Earthbound spirits are in a purgatory of sorts, bound to earth because of confusion or for some other pressing reason. Malik's action seemed to be the classic revenge plea.

Revenge was a petty emotion and did serve to keep a spirit bound to its previous life, which was a type of hell, compared to what was waiting for it.

Not that Malik didn't have good cause to be pissed. A young man in the prime of his life, brutally and likely painfully killed by his treacherous and, if she knew Ginger, two-timing, girlfriend for money that he'd like to have enjoyed also.

Bless wondered whether to tell Rick that his brother was around. Probably not. What purpose would it serve? His brother was a shadow of his former self, his former passions and mind distilled down to basic drives, sadness, anger, revenge. And his brother would never be able to reliably contact the average living person again. Bless had access to the other dimensions only by virtue of her powers.

Normally, she'd try to talk some sense into a sad spirit and send it on, but it wasn't wise to deal with an angry spirit. Malik would be satisfied when Ginger got her comeuppance.

Her sister was on a disastrous path, no matter what way you looked at it. It seemed as if something had broken away in her sister's mind. Poor Ginger had gone off the deep end and got all eviled out. She never was all that good, but the girl always had a healthy sense of self-preservation, and outright evil along with consorting with demons wasn't her style. Ginger had lost it, had fallen into the loony bin, had gone nutso, whatever way you wanted to put it. There was nothing to do to help her sister at this point, and that depressed Bless. The way things were, no matter what happened, there would be no wholly happy ending. But she knew that's the way life goes.

* * *

He knew just how to do it. Bless's **hips** rolled of their own volition and her fingers curled in Rick's hair. She'd been mortified when he first dived south. He kissed her there and said he loved the taste and smell of her. Then he proceeded to demonstrate the truth of his words.

Heaven knew she loved the feel of it. His steady sucking was building a volcano in the center of her. She gave herself over to it, trusting that it wouldn't crush her with its power. *Have mercy, darling*.

The magma crashed up inside the walls of the mountain, hot molten lava growing ever higher. The waves slammed, growing in strength and intensity until her entire body trembled, and every thought fled her mind.

Erupting, she spilled over, hot and quaking, her knees clutching the sides of his head. Waves so powerful they obliterated her, and it felt so good she screamed.

He slid into her, no longer able to hold back his own satisfaction, rock hard. He bucked against her, in that grinding motion she loved, his pelvis working against her clit on the down stroke. She was amazed that before she collected the scattered pieces of herself together, they started to burn again.

She rose to meet him eagerly. He met her eyes, brown against brown. He had the sight as far as telling when she was about to come. And he rolled and rocked inside her and took her all the way there.

Bless lay beside him, spent. She didn't want to sleep. She no longer dreamed about him, now that reality easily outpaced her dreams.

What replaced her former dreams of passion

was far worse. Now she dreamt of Ginger. Not her sister, Ginger, but another Ginger. A monstrous one, almost inhuman. One who allowed herself to be the playground of demons. The new Ginger was without mercy and what she sent were nightmares.

If Bless took a sleeping pill, she thankfully wouldn't dream at all, but then she might miss a message from Maris. She didn't know what to do.

Rick wondered whether to wake Bless. She was softly moaning in her sleep, but didn't seem acutely distressed. He decided to let her rest. She wasn't in too bad a state—he'd awakened too many times to her screaming, crying, and thrashing in her sleep.

She kept saying that they needed to go to Red Creek. The only reason they'd stayed in Atlanta so long was because Rick's mother begged them not to take her grandchild away and because of Rick's job. Bless acted like getting a new job was nothing. He knew better, and while he had a little savings, he bet her tune would change once their money got low. A man needs to work, and good jobs aren't a dime a dozen. He wasn't about to quit his to run to some backwoods Georgia town for no other reason than she wanted him there. She was the RN. She could get a job anywhere.

Now that time had passed since he'd witnessed Ginger levitating, he'd put the idea of demons and magic farther and farther from his mind. He preferred to concentrate on the concrete. Maybe it had been some trick of the light? No, he only wished that were so.

The investigation into Swank's murder was not

going well. Nobody could figure out how a woman, who'd recently undergone surgery, could overpower a young man, slice him open from stem to stern, and then disappear out of a busy hospital without a trace.

Rick shivered, remembering the scary light in Ginger's eyes. He was jumpy. He started at shadows and turned on the lights before he entered a darkened room. If he heard a strange noise, he wasn't about to investigate. As far as he was concerned, ghosts and demons could be tearing the roof off the sucker, as long as they stayed out of his space. There were some things that were simply too much for him to deal with.

17

Ginger paced like a lion in front of Bless. "So you think you've found love, sister of mine? What you've found is a sham and a tease. How are you going to keep a man? Have any of the aunts with power had a man as far back as you can remember? Does Praise have a man? Unless you change your destiny, you know what it will be."

"Sometimes we don't have all the answers, Ginger. If you'd trust in the universe, you'd see that things usually turn out for the good."

"Tell it to Cayenne, our mother, or Clove, our grandmother. They lived their lives and didn't buck the 'universe,' and what did they get for it? Labor pains and an opportunity to eat grave dirt before they were out of their prime."

Ginger sat and crossed her legs, her elaborate gold robes creasing. "I know what you want. Why don't you reach out your hand and will it into being? Think, Bless! A chance to have your own children, your own home. A chance to have Rick Jensen and never let him go."

Bless gave Ginger a sharp look. "Leave Rick out of it."

"Why should I?" Ginger pulled a cigarette pack out of a pocket of her gown and lit up. Bless crinkled her nose, but thankfully she couldn't smell unless she was in the flesh.

"He means a lot to you, doesn't he?" Ginger peered at Bless with narrowed eyes through the smoke. "You'd do almost anything to keep him safe."

"Don't even dream about it. You won't have to worry about concocting elaborate schemes to kill Glory because I'd kill you myself."

Ginger laughed. "I was right." She took a long draw. "His brother was basically a boring asshole, but he was great in the sack. I peeked in and saw Rick in action. Shit, I came myself just watching. Must be hereditary, ya think?"

Bless reached out to slap her, but her hand went right through Ginger's face.

"Temper, temper," Ginger said.

"Stay away from us," Bless said, her voice a growl. She'd strengthen the wards. At least she'd be warned of evil's approach.

"I wouldn't mind fucking Rick," Ginger said as if Bless hadn't said a word. "I could do it in memory of his sorry-ass brother. Then, I'll kill him too."

Ginger's laugh echoed as Bless lunged for her.

Bless woke shaking, in a cold sweat, Rick holding her and looking worriedly into her face.

"You're having nightmares almost nightly now. I'm going to take you to a doctor."

Bless got up to head for the bathroom. "It won't help," she said.

Rick was going to have to start believing in magic. Bless remembered the words of the prophecy. She knew that magic, combined with the power of their love in some way, was what it was going to take to defeat the darkness.

Bless wondered how a baby, a creature who could do basically nothing except eat and excrete, could mean so much to her? She hadn't given birth, she didn't have the hormones of motherhood circulating in her veins, yet she'd die without a second thought for little Glory.

She inhaled her baby scent and felt this peculiar happiness in the midst of everything going on, this happiness that came when it was just her and Glory, mother and daughter together. Glory wasn't her daughter, but it felt like it. Some special magic, mother magic, had settled on her and made it so.

It wasn't fair that Ginger could have and utterly disregard what she wanted so badly—to bear a child. A sliver of resentment slithered into Bless's heart, coiling and settling into a muck of bitterness.

The wards she set shrieked. Bless jumped to her feet and laid Glory in her crib, muttering a prayer for aid and protection. She heard the familiar sound of angelic swords being drawn from their sheaths around Glory.

Bless had barely gathered energies before she whirled to meet the threat breaking through the shields and somehow invading her home. She coalesced power for the kill, then hesitated. A child, barely three, toddled toward her.

"Help me," he said.

But the wards shrieked, heralding evil.

The child moved closer to Glory.

"Stop!" Bless yelled.

The child broke out in a run toward Glory. That was when Bless saw the pointed teeth no child could have. She lifted her arms, but it whirled and lashed out first, red fires of hell that she barely blocked. She screamed in agony as it burned her head to toe.

The child turned back to Glory. A knife appeared in the air and moved toward the baby.

"No," Bless whispered, and marshaled all her strength. A brilliant pink flare from her heart shot out and struck the demon. She saw the surprised look on the child's face before it dissolved into ash. The knife fell to the floor. Then the world faded to black and she felt the hardness of the floor as she collapsed.

Rick came home from work dog-tired. It had been one of those days that Murphy reigned over, everything going wrong that possibly could. He hated the politics, the constant BS, of a big-city police department as much as he loved detective work. His dream was to open a private detective agency, but that was easier said than done.

Especially now, when he was going to take on a family, a steady paycheck was more important than ever. Bless was bent on going to Red Creek. He was thinking that maybe he should let her go and drive there for the weekends. Bless kept telling him not to worry about the job, but damn, a job could be a terrible thing to waste.

"Bless? You home?" Usually delicious smells were emitting from the kitchen about now. He smiled to himself. She'd spoiled him already. "Bless?" He heard the baby in the den; why wasn't she answering?

He saw her crumpled in a heap at Glory's crib. "Bless!" he cried as he broke out in a run.

He cradled her in his arms as he pulled out his cell phone and dialed 911. She was so hot. And were those burns? How did she burn herself? She was already starting to blister. Bless was dark-skinned. For her to burn like this . . . He couldn't imagine.

He looked around him and quelled the urge to get out his cross and Star of David. Demons. Jesus Christ, he thought, and promptly turned it into a prayer.

"Where's Glory?" was the first thing Bless asked him.

"Right here." Rick moved the stroller so she could see. Bless exhaled in relief.

"You can't take your eyes off her. She's too vulnerable here. We have to get to Red Creek, where there's help."

"Bless, what happened?" he asked.

They were in one of those emergency room cubicles, drapes drawn. The doctors had been puzzled as he over Bless's sunburn, but determined that it wasn't life threatening. What they did find was that some vital electrolytes were depleted and they had some IV fluids dripping in now. He was told that as soon as they finished infusing, Bless could go home and would just have to care for her sunburn the usual way. Whatever that was.

"A demon entered to attack Glory."

"I thought you said evil couldn't come in unless invited."

Bless looked away, her expression drawn. "A gateway is often good enough, a weakness. It came in the guise of a child at a time when I was dwelling on motherhood . . . and children."

"You're not possibly blaming yourself?"

"Glory could have easily been killed."

"You were almost killed protecting her."

"But I wasn't . . . this time." Bless shifted. "I'm sore. What did the doctors say was wrong? When can I go?"

"Sunburn and electrolyte imbalance."

Bless nodded. "The demon hit me. I deflected it, a direct hit would have killed me, but I got burned. The electrolyte imbalance is interesting. I wasn't able to concentrate the energies the way I usually do, so I used a different source, one that was readily available, but one I never used before." She paused. "Heart fire."

"Heart fire?"

"Yes, the energies generated from my heart. I directly used my love for Glory to kill the demon and it worked. Cool, huh?"

Rick didn't know what to think, much less say. "Cool," he repeated.

Bless looked incredibly pleased with herself. "Yeah, wait until Maris hears. Apparently it throws body salts off, so afterwards I can just have some labs run—"

"Whoa. From what I hear, throwing body salts off can be extremely dangerous. They were quite concerned. And I don't want there ever to be another next time."

Bless didn't say anything, but he had a strong feeling that she was thinking it wasn't what he wanted that mattered.

"What are they going to do about the burn?" she asked.

"You're supposed to treat it like sunburn."

"So what does that mean?"

"I dunno. I've never been fool enough to get sunburned before."

"Neither have I," Bless said. "I didn't even think I could get sunburned. Now I guess I know I can. Damn, it hurts. *This* is what they risk for a tan? You got to be kidding."

"I guess we can look up treatment on the Internet," Rick mused.

Bless was staring at the peeling skin on her forearms in fascination. "Sunburn, sheesh," she said.

Rick had asked a nurse and she'd directed him to the hospital pharmacy, where they gave him several sunburn treatment creams he could purchase. He chose one, and called in an order for Chinese food. Bless was determined to go to Red Creek, but in her condition it wouldn't be tonight. She needed to rest. She assured him that the house would be safe from demon invasion for the time being.

He didn't know how to tell her that he wasn't going to Red Creek with her, but tonight, over the Chinese food, he guessed he'd figure it out.

Glory lay in her stroller, gurgling and shrieking in baby glee over some imaginary bauble. "That's right, darlin'," he said, bending over and smiling at her.

Then suddenly he saw a glittery, rainbow-colored, butterfly-appearing thing over the baby's head.

It was gone by the time he'd raced with the stroller back to the ER. He was near babbling himself when he tried to tell Bless what happened.

Then he *felt* something from Bless. She closed

her eyes for a moment and he felt something wrapping around her like cotton candy.

It just wasn't his day.

"Just calm down, Rick, and tell me exactly what you saw. There's no evil with malevolent intentions toward us or the baby near here right now."

"It was a rainbow butterfly. It didn't look really real. It was about as big as her head."

"Did you feel any fear? Think carefully. I know you were alarmed but was there any fear?"

He paused, remembering. "No, I wasn't scared of it. More like freaked out."

"And the baby laughed?"

"Yes."

Bless relaxed. "I think it was okay. I would have sensed an attack. I think it was only one of her protectors playing with her."

"Protectors?"

"I suppose you'd call them guardian angels. She has quite a few. And believe me, she needs every one."

Rick's eyebrows shot up. Guardian angels? His world was tilting sideways and he supposed it wouldn't ever straighten up.

18

Bless dug out a big, juicy shrimp with her chopsticks. "Mmmm," she said, her eyes closed with satisfaction. "That's good."

"I'm happy you're enjoying it. I guess this is a good time to talk to you about something I have on my mind."

Bless opened her eyes. "Okay," she said.

"It's about going to Red Creek." He sighed.

"Okay," she said.

"I know it's really important to you and all." He paused.

"Okay?" Bless said.

"But I don't think I'm going to be able to go with you," he said in a rush. There, it was done.

Bless put down the carton of Chinese food. "Why is that?" she asked.

"I don't want to lose my job. There are only so many police departments and so many detective positions in Atlanta. A man needs to be responsible."

"You know, Rick, I'd agree with you in a heart-beat if that job was what you really wanted. But you know that job isn't your heart's desire."

His breath caught. Police work not his heart's desire?

His father had worked his way up from the beat to the city hall and he was bound and determined that his sons follow in his footsteps and be cops. An honorable family tradition, he said. They'd had it drummed into them as soon as they could understand.

There wasn't any question about what he would do. His dad was almost disappointed when the school counselor told him it would be a shame if Rick didn't go to college. He grudgingly allowed Rick to put off the Police Academy if he majored in criminal justice.

Malik followed the same path, but in college, he'd indulged his love for computers. He entered the force and lasted for two years before he trans-ferred to the information technology department in city hall. Dad had a fit.

His father was an extremely loving man, but old-fashioned and set in his ways. It was that love that made his sons strive to please him no matter what the demand. Rick remembered many joyful times growing up with his dad—and his brother. He swallowed the lump in his throat that never quite went away. Hard to realize that they were both gone.

Rick had never had a real love for police work; rather it was a job, a duty, something to please his father. But how did Bless know his heart? He looked at her in query.

"Can you imagine meeting somebody that you

feel that you've known forever? That not only you know their heart, that you know almost everything about them?" she asked.

He answered truthfully, "No, I can't."

Bless stared into the carton of Chinese food. "Maybe one day you will." She picked up her glass of wine and sipped. "You need to come with me. I can't tell you exactly why, but it's urgent that you do so. The job is inconsequential by comparison."

She put down the glass and clasped her hands together. "Rick, I'm asking you to trust me."

"I give up my job for what, Bless? For magic, spells, demons, and whispers of a coming Armageddon I can do nothing to control? This isn't my world and I'm not sure I want it to be."

"We can't help what is," Bless said in a low voice.

They sat beside each other in silence for a while, a standoff, the Chinese food growing cold. Then a tinkle of something like bells chimed off to the right and Bless sprang to her feet.

Rick followed. "What's going on?" he asked.

"Something is here. But the wards haven't sounded. No evil has approached," she said.

A shimmer grew in the living room and solidified to a handsome young black man with a big grin. "You better listen to her, bro'," he said.

Rick stared at him, gasped, and fainted clean away.

"Oops, I think big brother has about had enough," Malik said. "But that should get him to Red Creek." Then he faded away.

Bless frowned. Why did Malik want Rick in Red Creek too? Since Malik was stuck on one intention, undoubtedly he thought Rick had to be there for his revenge to be carried out.

At least, for the time being, she and Malik were on the same page. She wished she could do something to help the earthbound spirit as she fanned Rick's unconscious form. Maybe soon.

"Malik?" Rick said as he came to.

"He's gone."

"Where did he go? Malik!" he called, sitting up.

"I don't think he's coming back. It took a huge effort to do what he did."

Rick rubbed his eyes, stood, and walked over to where Malik had manifested. "Am I going crazy?" he muttered. "What's going on?"

"Your brother Malik is earthbound. He's bound to the earth by a desire for revenge for his untimely death. He came to you at this time because he wants you to go to Red Creek."

"Earthbound? Well, why didn't he come to his own damn funeral? Why didn't he comfort his mother?"

"He can't be perceived by most humans. What could he do for his mother? He was still dead, his body in the ground. And he *was* at his funeral. I saw him."

"Where is he now?" Rick asked through stiff lips.

"In the cemetery."

"You know what I mean."

"He's on another plane or in another dimension, however you'd like to term it. It looks like here, pretty much, but it doesn't change. Nothing grows, nothing lives, nothing dies. It's dark, gray, and there's nobody else there. He wanders that world. Occasionally he can see a flash of our world here, or perceive something or somebody that he has an emotional connection to. With great effort, he might be able to manifest between the worlds and be perceived here by sensitive individuals. He must have connected with your feeling of resistance of going to Red Creek. He would want you to go if he thought that was the way he would get his revenge."

Rick turned away. "I'm going to bed now," he said. "I have a headache."

Bless watched him walk away, and she ached at the turmoil inside him. He'd truly had enough. He needed some space, and although she wanted to touch and comfort him, she had the wisdom to grant his need.

The next morning, she was up making coffee and preparing breakfast. Rick came down late for him, around nine. She guessed he wasn't going into the station today.

He got a cup of coffee and sat at the table. "I called my boss and told him I had to take some time off. I said my brother's death was tearing me up. He said he understood. I have an indefinite leave." He gave a wry grin. "I never realized that I was so dispensable."

Bless touched his arm. "It's just a job, honey."

"Are you going to say, it's just money, honey, when we don't have any?"

"Abundance is a gift of the universe if you expect it to be there."

Rick said nothing, but Bless sensed he was holding back from lavish eye rolling. Rick wasn't exactly a New Age type of guy. But he'd come around.

"I think we should pack lightly to head out to Red Creek, don't you?" she said.

"Yeah."

Bless got a cup of coffee and settled across the

table from him. "First, I want to tell you about Red Creek and my family."

She started at what she thought was the beginning, the Middle Passage. Her voice broke when she told of her mother's death. Then afterward, the living, the caretaking, the dying, and the loneliness in between. She must have spoken a long time because, when she looked up, he was looking at her as if he knew her. Really knew her.

"Remember when you asked me if we . . ." His voice trailed away.

"Yes, I remember."

"When you were talking, it was as if I remembered you. And what came to me was that we'd been separated all this time, and now we're finally together again, as we're meant to be."

It slipped into place and clicked. Through the ages, had he been by her side in one guise or another until cruel fate tore them apart for lifetimes?

Had her loneliness run deep because she'd been missing the other half of herself, her twin flame?

Her head bowed when she remembered what Ginger said. Her choices could condemn her to lifetimes more of that terrible loneliness. Was she doing the right thing? What could be more important than this man sitting right here? Maybe she should walk away from Glory for the chance to remain in his arms?

He reached out and touched her hand. "No matter what, we'll always be together. Seeing my brother helps me to realize that death is meaningless. Nothing but a change in location."

He sounded like Maris.

"I don't want to make the wrong choice and lose this. It's like a miracle, do you understand? I have been so alone." To her dismay, tears were rolling down her cheeks. Lately she was always crying or deliriously happy, on a mountain range of emotion, where before her emotional vista had been an arid plain.

He took out a tissue and handed it to her. She blew her nose.

"Bless, you helped make the choice about the job easier. You've always been so clear. Do what you know is right. That way you can't go wrong in the long run."

In the long run. The long run could mean lifetimes. She didn't want to spend any more lifetimes separated from her other half, all alone.

Glory was upstairs napping after her morning bottle. "Take me upstairs and make love to me, Rick," she said. "Hold me and never let me go."

19

Rick followed Bless on the highway to Red Creek. She kept looking out her rearview mirror, some part of her afraid that in the next glance he'd be gone.

Afraid?

Fear was the opposite of love, the sire of hatred, the gateway to darkness. *Yea, though I walk through the valley of the shadow of death, I will fear no evil . . .*

How could she allow fear to take hold in her heart? Rick had told her what she knew well: Do what you know is right, and trust in the good to follow. The ones she loved most cautioned her against the fear of death. *Nothing but a change of location.*

But she'd been bound up in fear, a gateway for darkness. She looked in her rearview mirror, where she could see Glory busily chewing on a toy. She loved the child, no doubt.

She took a breath and inhaled. And she loved Rick, always had and always would. Nothing could change that. Most important was who she was and who she would always be—a worker of light, not darkness.

Bless drove on toward Red Creek with a new resolve.

Rick pulled up behind her. He got out of the car and glanced at Glory. "Did she do all right?"

"She did great. Needs changing though."

He craned his head up at the old house. "Wonderful house—old, isn't it?"

"Our family has lived here since the late seventeen hundreds."

"I didn't think they allowed blacks to own property here back then."

"They didn't. It belonged to our owners. Their family line died out and it came down to us. We sisters always worked their kitchen and nursery."

"You are probably some of the few blacks in this country who have any idea of your lineage that far back. Seems as if you should be in the history books somewhere."

"No, we never made it into any history books. We had humble jobs and minded our own business."

Maids, mammies, cooks, bedwarmers to white men, what else could a black woman do until recently? She wondered if the heady flush of opportunity was what made Ginger chafe so. In the days before, a woman such as Ginger had no hope of excitement and less of glamour in her life. An early death might not have looked so bad from Ginger's viewpoint in the nineteenth century.

The circle turns.

"Let's go on in," Bless said.

"The baby!" Aunt Praise pulled open the door and ran from the porch with surprising speed for someone of her age and size. She peered at Glory in her carrier. "She's so beautiful, Bless."

"Isn't she? Aunt Praise, this is Rick Jensen, Glory's uncle. Rick, Praise Sanderson."

Praise shook Rick's hand and assessed him head to toes. "Nice to meet you, Rick," she said. Then she turned to Bless and winked.

Embarrassed, Bless hurried into the house with Glory while Praise showed Rick where to put their bags. Miriam was sitting in her rocking chair looking out the window at a bird. "See your new niece, Aunt Miriam?"

She seemed so like Maris, Bless half expected her to look up, smile, and ask her how's it been going? But Miriam did none of those things. She didn't acknowledge her, just kept rocking, rocking, vacant eyes on the bird, mouth open. Where was Miriam now, Bless wondered? What worlds was she visiting, what adventures was she having?

Her shell sat in this world, nothing, while her spirit soared.

Bless widened her perceptions in preparation to cleansing the atmosphere of the house. She frowned as she perceived the petty negative residues of Aunt Praise's work. It would have to stop at once. Glory would be in danger.

Rick entered the room followed by Praise. Bless wondered if her aunt had put them together or in separate bedrooms. It would be interesting to see how psychic her aunt truly was.

"You have done a lot of work on this house," Rick said.

"It's continually ongoing. If you stay here any amount of time, something is certain to need fixing. Are you handy?" Praise asked.

"Not really," he said.

"We have plenty of books," Praise replied.

Rick looked nervous.

Bless was changing Glory on a mat and tickling her brown tummy. She deftly got the diaper on and settled Glory in the bassinet. "I'm going to wash my hands and fix her a bottle before I put her down for a nap. Aunt Praise, I need to talk to you. It's serious. I'll make us a pot of tea."

"A tea talk, huh?" Bless heard Praise saying to Rick. "She must want to get on to me about something. Hey, Bless," she called. "Be sure and phone that hospital. They've been driving me crazy ringing the phone off the hook about when you're going to be back."

The hospital would have to wait. She had a baby to care for and demon fighting to do.

She washed her hands, warmed water to the perfect degree of warmness in the microwave, and then mixed it with Glory's formula. She had this mommy thing down. The tea kettle whistled and she poured boiling water into the pot with orange clove tea. Then she put it on a tray with three cups, saucers, spoons, and the sugar jar so Aunt Praise could get her tea as sweet as she liked it. Sweet is good when one is being read the riot act.

She took the tray out first, and returned with the bottle. "Can I feed her?" Aunt Praise asked.

"Sure," Bless said, handing Glory over. Nothing can mellow a person out more than an armful of sweet-smelling baby.

She hated it when Praise got angry. Mad Praise

made for a miserable household. She definitely didn't believe in suffering in silence.

Bless cleared her throat. "Aunt Praise, you're going to have to stop your charm and psychic business now that Glory is here. I told you how that sort of thing lowers the overall vibration and opens the way for evil to enter."

Praise was cooing to Glory and gave no indication of having heard a word Bless had said.

"Aunt Praise?"

"I know, child. I'm going to quit. I only wanted to get some money laid up before you came. Isn't she cute? Look, she smiled at me!"

Well, that was easier then she thought. Bless leaned back on the sofa and sipped her tea. "She put us together in a room," Rick whispered in her ear, trying to hold back his grin.

A little while later, Glory was asleep and they were seated around the kitchen table, a war council of sorts.

"I've set wards. They'll warn if evil approaches from any angle and also repel it to some extent," Praise said.

"The house is sealed and cleansed of negative energies," Bless added.

"Uh, I unpacked," Rick said after a pause. "I feel kind of useless."

"You're not useless," Praise said. "There's a strong reason that you're here with us, or you wouldn't be."

"She's right," Bless said.

"It's that I'm a take-action sort of guy and it's difficult to figure out what sort of action to take in these circumstances. Set wards, cleanse atmospheres? Beat up invisible things? All out of my ken."

Bless considered Rick. He wasn't going to do well sitting around. He needed a project. "The windows and doors need weather stripping. I know Aunt Praise didn't get to it without me around and I meant to do it right before I left but—that's what we really need done." She looked at him expectantly.

He raised an eyebrow. "Okay. But one thing I want to do also. I want to study about demons and wards and all this esoteric stuff you're constantly telling me about. You have books?"

Bless gazed at him in amazement. What a great idea he had. "I have books."

"All right then."

"Are you two done?" Praise asked, "Because I have something to tell you about our family, about your mother, that I haven't shared with you before. But it's past time." They looked at her expectantly.

"Your mother was like Ginger, beautiful and brash. She had you, then slipped into a postpartum depression. She got pregnant six months later. When she had Miriam, she briefly came back to her old self. Then six months later she again got pregnant. She was near suicidal, and when Ginger was born, she wouldn't hold her, wouldn't look at her.

"She started hearing voices. She didn't tell me about them yet, but I knew something had changed. She started the study and art of magic, because she always envied my powers. The atmosphere grew foul and evil. Somehow on the way, her magic turned dark. She got it into her head that if she killed the babies, she could save herself."

Praise stopped and closed her eyes. "Oh Lord, forgive me," she said, her voice cracking.

Bless grew alarmed at the tears flowing down Praise's face. "What's wrong? What happened?"

Rick handed her a tissue. He was real good at that. Aunt Praise wiped her eyes. "I had to kill her. We always do, generation after generation. Or you see what would happen—she'd kill all the babies."

20

"Does Ginger know that story?" Bless asked Aunt Praise.

"I doubt it."

"I saw symbols of black magic in her room."

Praise frowned. "It's too early. She isn't supposed to go there until after the third child."

Rick cleared his throat. "How did you . . . um, kill Ginger's mother?" he asked.

Praise rubbed her hand across her brow. "I wasn't always the way I am now. When I was younger, I was more like Bless, powerful. I could heal. I connected with the ethers and touched Cayenne, drew her life force out and passed it back to the elements."

Rick exhaled. "You realize that if your aunt had said anything less ridiculous, I'd be obligated to arrest her. Or at least turn her in. But by any account that's loony."

Praise looked offended. Bless looked relieved. "Thanks, Rick," Bless said.

"Thank him for what?" Praise said to her niece. "He just called me loony."

"He said it sounded loony, and it would to an outsider. You know that. He's a cop and you just confessed to a murder. Think about it."

Praise thought. "Oh," she said.

"On her death certificate, it says she died of cardiac arrest—that her heart simply stopped. That was their best guess, they really didn't know," Bless said.

Praise looked away, her face drawn.

Bless felt confused and conflicted. She sensed the utter truth in Praise's words. She also sensed the darkness. Praise had caused a human death. When she killed her sister, Cayenne, she crossed over to the same side.

Suddenly Bless felt a whole lot less safe.

"It's in you too," Aunt Praise was telling her.

"What?"

"The death. You know you're going to have to do it. For some reason the timing is off, but to save the baby, you're going to have to kill Ginger."

"I'm going to destroy the demons she's using and I'm going to stop Ginger. But I'm not killing anybody."

Praise cocked her head. "Don't you understand? You have no choice. The demons are using her, not the other way around. They need a willing human conduit."

"How do I know that wouldn't be you?" Bless asked, her voice soft.

Praise's face crumpled and she started to cry again.

"This has been enough for one day," Rick said. "I suggest we turn in for an early night."

Bless had to agree. She'd been waking with the baby through the nights and she was bone tired, soul weary. "That's a good idea," she said.

* * *

Praise had settled Rick in her room and it was a good thing because he wanted every book she had on the occult and the magical arts. Many were in the bookcases that lined the walls of her bedroom. She brushed her teeth, put on a comfy nightgown, and curled up, leaving Rick propped up on extra pillows on the other side of the bed, his head in a book. She closed her eyes and hoped she wouldn't dream.

It was way too much to hope for.

"The old bag finally told you," Ginger said.

Bless said nothing.

"We're always surprised to find out what's inside us." She chuckled. "You know what I'm talking about, Miss High and Mighty. We're all the same. You're a killer too."

"I don't think so."

"Only because this time you're not going to get the goddamned opportunity. I'm gonna get you first. Promise." Ginger winked at her and was gone.

Bless was on the hill under the willow tree with Maris.

"You thought you needed me?" Maris asked.

"So much," Bless said. "I don't know what to do next. I feel like I'm in limbo. I hate the waiting. And about Praise . . . I don't know what to think."

A sweet breeze blew through the willow branches. "You don't need me. You need to trust your heart. You have what you need. Stay the course and things will turn out for the good."

"How can I kill Ginger?"

"Do you think you have to kill Ginger?"

"I don't believe I should take human life."

"Then don't." Maris patted her hand. "You have what you need. Trust in it."

And then Maris faded away to memory.

Bless was in the kitchen washing dishes, the radio on the counter playing a catchy beat. Rick had his nose in a book, as usual. He was like a student cramming for finals, devouring book after book. Glory was sleeping. Newborns seemed to do that a lot. Bless hardly got to play with her. But what was important was that the baby was safe.

Bless ran through their defenses in her mind. They were strong. And she was a demon slayer, one of the few in the world alive today, she guessed. She whirled in a reenactment of the move she'd done on that yellow-eyed demon. It didn't come off quite the same when she was in the body, but it was pretty good. She kicked and punched to the beat of the music. Yeah, she was Bless, the big, bad, black demon slayer. Buffy, you better watch yo'self, there's a new girl in town. Bless giggled to herself.

"Having fun?"

She spun to the sight of Rick leaning in the doorway watching her, hands in his pockets. How embarrassing.

Her face heated like red-hot coals and she turned back to the dishwater and plunged her hands in. A few seconds later she felt his warm body behind her, his lips at her neck. "You have rhythm, woman. You turn me on."

She could say that he was doing the same for her, his erection pressing into the small of her back. She could feel the moisture between her legs as his hands cupped her breasts, his thumbs massaging her nipples. She pressed back against him, and one of his hands dropped to the waistband of her jeans and deftly unsnapped it.

He slipped his hand inside her panties, and his fingers found her moist button and rubbed it in rhythm with her nipple. She ground against his hardness, starting to breathe hard. She wanted him to do her right here at the kitchen sink. Then modesty kicked in. "Praise might come home from the store any moment," she said.

"Then we should retire to the bedroom right away," Rick said, grasping her by her waist from behind, holding her snugly against his erection and leading her to the bed.

They fell on the bed, pulling and tugging at each other's clothes. Bless's fingers eagerly unzipped Rick's jeans and his hard cock sprang free. She grasped it and guided it to her entry, her legs parting and hugging his slim hips.

He plunged into her and she stifled a shout, not wanting to wake Glory, but oh, he felt so good. He gave it to her hard, bucking and grinding, her vagina filled to the hilt with his heat.

Don't stop. He moved in a rotating movement that about sent her crazy, as the head moved inside her.

"Look at me," he commanded. She looked into his black-coffee eyes. "I'm going to take you there. I'm bringing it now."

He wasn't lying because quivering, uncontrollable tremors started all over her body. She could do nothing but give in to his power. Her eyes started to close.

"Come to me, baby," he said, kissing her neck and thrusting his organ deep. "Don't close your eyes."

Her eyes were open, but she couldn't see a damn

thing. She was coming hard, pouring out and scattering into tiny pieces that she didn't know would ever come back together.

He stiffened, gushing into her, joining earthy essences into one.

Spent, they lay together panting, limbs entangled, hearts steadying.

Bless felt the soupy stickiness between her legs and wanted to swear. They completely forgot the condom, just like the damn things didn't exist. She disengaged herself from him and rolled off the bed into the bathroom.

She got under the too hot water of the shower and scrubbed with a soapy wash towel. She guessed the lack of a condom was no disaster. She doubted if Rick had any dread disease, and she knew if she asked, he'd get tested readily. And as far as getting pregnant . . . it would be the best thing that ever happened to her.

She bit her lip at the treacherous thought. They took being together for granted, but neither had brought up marriage yet and that's what babies go with. She was being premature—no, they were, because the lack of a condom was as much his oversight as it was hers.

As if he knew she had him on her mind, Rick drew the shower curtain aside and stepped in beside her. "I need one, too," he said.

Showered and dressed in fresh clothes, Bless looked over the pile of occult books Rick had stacked on the dining room table. "Have you read all of these?"

"I've at least skimmed most of them."

"Learned anything?" She tried to sound nonchalant, but it was important to her that he understood at least a part of her world.

Rick crossed his arms and leaned back in his chair. "I need to understand about Malik. I can't seem to find anything enlightening in these books about life after death; it's all about magical arts. Where is he and how can I reach him, help him, or bring him back?"

Disappointment touched her. Malik. Rick wasn't interested in prophecies or demons or Armageddon, but something that his eyes had seen and something far closer to his heart.

"You can't bring back the dead," she said. "It's not possible, never has been."

"These books refer to it."

"They refer to a lie, an illusion. Once the soul has left the body, all you have left is meat, and rotting meat at that."

Rick flinched. "I saw him and you did too. Don't lie to me. You also said you saw him at his funeral. What did you see? I saw a man, not some wraith floating around in white sheets. There has to be some mistake."

"What we saw was something like a film projection against the air, an image only. It was a thought form, Malik's thought form, so yes, it was dressed the way he customarily dressed, with the appearance he customarily had. If he remains earthbound, in time he will forget his prior human body and his appearance will gradually change."

"I never believed in ghosts. Do you know why, Bless?"

Surprised by the undertone of bitterness in his voice, she shook her head.

"If people lived on after this life, how could they bear to leave?" he continued. "We hurt so much to lose them, so wouldn't their pain be greater? Wouldn't the world be so crowded with ghosts you couldn't turn around without bumping into one? If people could stick around after they die, why would my father have ever left?"

Bless sighed. She started to speak, but he raised his hand to stop her.

"Do you know why my father would never have left? Because he was such a controlling son of a bitch, if there was some way he could stick around and rule our lives after death, he surely would have done so."

After his speech Rick waited with an expectant air. "That was the ultimate test to prove that there's no life after death," he said. "If Dad heard me speak so disrespectfully of him, he would have come back just to kick my ass from one end of this house to the other."

"For most people, after they die, the veil is lifted," Bless said.

Rick raised a quizzical brow.

"The soul remembers all the other lives he's lived. The past one and the connections he had there were just one life of many. He remembers other souls that he's known for eons and joyfully reunites with them. The place he's returning to is familiar and beautiful in comparison with the hard school of earth. He reflects on lessons learned. There is no desire to go back because everything is viewed through an entirely different perception, a far richer one."

"So why isn't Malik floating around in paradise then?"

"Some people never allow the veil to be lifted because they are bound to this world in some way or fixed on the circumstances of their death. Malik is fixated on the injustice of his death, anger, and revenge. He can't move on in that state."

"Why did he show himself?"

"I told you once, he wants you here in Red Creek. He knows that Ginger is coming eventually and he thinks he will be able to work out his revenge through you in some way."

Rick drummed his fingers on the table. "This has been a nice relaxing interlude, but I can't stay in Red Creek lounging around forever. I need to support myself. I have some savings, but the bills don't magically stop. And I really don't get the urgent point of my presence. We can still see each other." He straightened. "I wanted to talk to you about getting a job in Atlanta and staying with me. That makes a lot more sense. You're an RN. You could have a job within half an hour, I bet."

"Glory's safer here."

"Why is that? You can do abracadabra crap just as well in Atlanta."

"You'll be real thankful for abracadabra crap when it's saving your ass," Bless said sharply.

Rick said nothing, his fingers thrumming. Bless went to put on the teapot, the tension between them deep and heavy.

That was a case of her mouth outrunning her brain. That usually didn't happen. But she was angry, scared, and uncertain all together. Why was it so important that they remain here in Red Creek? Praise was a help, but now that Bless knew she was a murderess, she could end up a profound hindrance.

What could she say to Rick? That she knew in her bones, in every cell of her body, that all three of them needed to stay in Red Creek together. That certainly Glory's life depended on it and probably theirs too—and maybe the fate of the world.

She returned to the dining room with two cups

of tea, and Rick was looking pensive. "I'm sorry." He waved at the books. "All this is so beyond what I'm used to. And it's so soon after my brother's death. It's tearing me up inside, girl. I'd give anything to talk to him, to know what happened to him. At least I could get some closure. Can you do anything to help me?"

Bless's eyes narrowed. What she needed was for Rick to truly believe in magic. Then his perceptions would open and he would see the reality of the threat. She didn't know how to begin to convince him of the worlds beyond worlds and the possibilities outside of his senses. But maybe his brother Malik could.

21

The November wind was sharp and blustery and the midnight hour was close. Bless shivered in her heavy coat. Alarm bells had gone off in her head when she decided to summon Malik's spirit in the house. Do it outside near running water, her intuition said, and Bless always minded her intuition.

She and Rick stood in a stand of pine trees by a slow-moving creek. She needed none of the physical trappings of a medium. The timing, midnight, was conducive and the right state of mind essential. But she was anxious. This was not her thing at all; it was Praise's territory. She wished Aunt Praise were with her now, but she dared not leave Glory unguarded.

Bless took deep breaths to calm and steady her mind. "Come here, Rick. Stand in front of me and hold my hands."

"What do you want me to do?" he asked.

"Just close your eyes."

She said a prayer of protection and, shifting to

that other place where spirits dwell, sent out a mental beacon of her call for Malik.

She returned and said, "Malik, come forth," out loud, primarily for Rick's benefit.

There was a faint chime like the one she had heard before, an odor of . . . was that hot chicken wings?

"Malik?" Rick whispered. "He always loved chicken wings."

The sharp smell was growing stronger. She guessed it was hot sauce, but she'd never heard of the like as far as manifestations went.

"You called?" a voice to the left said.

Rick loosened his grip and Bless tightened hers. "Don't let go of my hands," she said.

"Malik! What happened, man? Is there anything we can do? Any way we can . . . bring you back?"

Suddenly the metallic smell of blood overpowered the smell of hot sauce. "The bitch stuck a knife in my back like she was butchering a pig. The pain, oh, the pain. I screamed for mercy but she kept sticking it in again and again." Choking and gasping sounds.

"Malik, be at peace," Bless said.

"Bitch, I can't be at peace. Not until she and hers die the death you deserve!"

You deserve? Bless wondered.

Then she felt a sharp pain in her back and she screamed, bending, but trying to maintain contact with Rick. But Rick had released her hand at the moment of her scream.

Quickly she grasped power from the sky and protected herself with a shield of dark blue flames.

"A branch just flew into your back!" Rick yelled.

He shielded her with his body and the branches dropped to the ground before striking him.

"Malik, no!" he roared.

"Rick, take my hands, now!" Fear crawled through her body like unclean snakes. She peered through the worlds and saw Malik dart into his brother's body.

Rick crumpled into the dirt; it was too late.

"I command you to release him, Malik," Bless ordered.

Rick's eyes popped open. "You wouldn't have any hot wings on hand, would you?" he asked.

Bless moved into that other plane and screamed her demon battle cry. She'd been coached to use it to collect her energies for the attack, but it was a good release for sheer fury.

She whipped into Rick's body and lifted her leg and kicked Malik's skinny spirit rear so hard that he bounced off a tree instead of sailing through it.

Malik lay on the ground flat on his back. "Ouch, that hurt. I didn't think anything could hurt anymore. How did you do that?"

"Your purpose in coming here, fool," Bless growled, "is to convince Rick to stay in Red Creek and that supernatural phenomena exist. It's not to kill me, possess him, or to eat chicken wings, savvy? 'Cause if not, if you think that hurt, wait until I get through with you—you'll wish you could die again."

She lifted her leg as if to kick him. "Don't kick me again, okay?" he said. "I savvy. I just forgot you weren't your sister. Things get a little fuzzy here. I'm not thinking too well."

And he would think worse and remember less as time passed. "You need to move on up out of here,

Malik. I'm sure you've heard of heaven. There's a place like that if you'd only let it take you. Go toward the light."

A frown crossed his face. "That bitch killed me," he said.

"We got that. If you want to settle the score, Rick is going to have to stay in Red Creek, right?"

"Right."

"So make it so," Bless snapped. That branch in her back had been painful.

She moved back to her body. Rick was frantically trying to examine her superficial wound and figure out why she wasn't responding to him. "I'm back."

"Thank God, you're speaking. I was about to call 911. But your pulse was steady and your color good. The branch barely penetrated your skin."

"I went into a trance for a brief time. I'm sorry, but it was necessary."

"Rick." Malik had manifested visibly this time. He sat cross-legged on the ground a few feet from his brother. "I'm sorry, bro. It was the thought of tasting a chicken wing again. It made me crazy."

"Sorry for what? What are you talking about?"

"Never mind. You have to stay in Red Creek so the bitch can die. That's what you can do for me." He gave a grimace of a smile. "You can call it a deathbed wish."

With those words he was gone.

Bless's back throbbed. She hated messing with ghosts.

After Bless filled him in on everything that happened with Malik that he couldn't perceive, Rick scarcely said a word on the walk back to the house.

Bless supposed that meeting with one's dead brother was enough to drain a person. It certainly had drained her.

It wasn't until they were settled under the blankets, after he'd cleaned and dressed the minor wound on her back, that Rick spoke. "Is the house secure?" he asked.

"Secure as can be," Bless said.

"How secure can a house be against . . ." Rick hesitated, obviously not wanting to say the words. "Spirits and demons?"

"Fairly secure. It's hard to be sure. It's not walls that protect so much as the intentions and inclinations of the people inside."

"You and I are all right, but what about Praise?" Rick asked.

"That's my question too. That's why the news that she killed my mother shook me up."

"So we should leave."

"No, something tells me we have to stay here."

Rick looked exasperated. "What tells you all these things, Bless? You seem to base an awful lot on vague inner promptings that could be generated by some other internal motive entirely."

"I've had the sight all my life. It's more than vague inner promptings. And when I ignore it, things always turn out badly."

"If you say so. After what I experienced today, it's hard not to believe you. How does it feel?"

She hesitated. Could she tell him in a way he'd understand? "Sometimes it's a thought, not mine, but from outside, like it's inserted. Sometimes it's a voice or a vision. But most of the time, it's this certainty of what is, similar to how you know that if you put your hand on a hot stove, it'll burn."

Rick's brow crinkled. "I feel helpless and I don't

like this feeling. I need something to do. You told me that Malik took control of my body and I didn't realize it. You had to save me. What if—"

Bless touched her fingers to his lips. "There is no what if. What will be, simply is. Things are as they are and our main job is to accept them."

Rick took her fingers in his and intertwined them briefly with his before he released them. "Good night," he said and turned off the lamp on his side of the bed. Bless did the same, and lay in the dark listening to him breathe. He was awake also; she could feel his unsettled emotions. She wanted to reach out to him, but his back was turned to her, his face buried in his pillow.

"As far as closure goes, that really sucked," Rick's voice drifted from the pillow.

How could she disagree? Suck it did. Bless felt guilt settle somewhere in the region of her gut. Maybe she could have thought of another way.

"It's nice to know he's conscious anyway. Sort of. He's changed." He paused. "I suppose dying would do that to a person."

"It generally does, Rick."

He turned his bedside lamp back on, and moved to his side facing her. "Bro is in a terrible state. I was going to suggest that he drop in and pay Mama his respects; you know, ease her mind. But after I saw him, I knew it would be a bad idea. We'd be burying her too."

"Yes, that would be a bad idea. Malik is an earth-bound spirit. He's going to lose more and more of his earthly personality and memories the longer he stays, but the veil isn't lifted so he can't remember who he really is as souls do when they leave the earth. He'll eventually be like an old scratched record replaying a few notes over and over. You know, like those ghosts who reenact their deaths or some dramatic event at the same spot repeatedly? They're stuck."

"We have to send him on to—you did say it was heaven, right? He's already two short of all his marbles."

"Once this is resolved, and it will be eventually, he'll move on to the next plane."

Rick lay on his back and stared at the ceiling. "Malik wants me to stay here too, but for what? It's getting to me to have nothing to do but think about things I can't begin to understand and don't know if I want to. I'm a cop. If there's a threat, I want to face it head on, not lie around eating down-home cooking, reading, and gaining weight, waiting for you to save me."

That was the crux of the problem, Bless knew. It was a man thing. He felt he couldn't help her in the demon butt-whupping department. Worse, he knew that he had to count on her to save him if need be.

The good thing was at least he could acknowledge the fact, but the bad thing was that it was true. He had no powers. That made no sense, considering what she suspected. "Do me a favor and touch my palm to yours," she said.

He sat up and touched their hands together, fingers outstretched. "What are you going to do?" he asked.

"I'm going to perceive our auras."

She gazed at their hands, their auras dancing and flickering around the physical forms of their fingers. The colors were different. His were human, good, healthy, and energetic, but without mysticism. Her aura was violet and gold, shot with white, the color of a mage, a wizard, a mystic—somebody infused with power.

But there was something strange in the pattern. They matched exactly, one's auric flares and movements a mirror of the other. Uncanny, like matching fingerprints. He was undoubtedly her twin flame, the divided half of her soul from the time of creation. But why did he have no power? Why did she have it all?

"Have you ever had any attraction towards the occult or mysticism? Ever dreamed dreams that came true, heard voices, or saw things you couldn't explain?" she asked.

He raised an eyebrow. "I've never had any interest in the occult whatsoever. I don't even read my horoscope. As far as hearing voices and the rest, if something like that ever happened, I'd run, not walk, to the nearest shrink."

"I believe you're my twin flame. See?" She showed him a birthmark on her right thigh that exactly matched his in size and shape. "Our auras match too."

"And? What's a twin flame?"

She needed to suggest that his reading material include some of the more elementary esoteric texts, and less on the magical arts. She was going to have to start at the beginning.

"Our souls were neither male nor female at the time of creation. The creator split us into polarities. One could be male, the other female, or vice versa. The point is that these two souls were once one, part of a whole. They are identical except for the polarity. They aren't always embodied at the same time, but when they are, they are always of the opposite sex. Since they can occupy any space in that time, or be any age, one twin flame rarely meets another in the flesh. But we have."

She paused. Rick was studying her. Did his eyes look slightly glazed?

"Since we are identical," she continued, "it's strange that I have power and you don't. There must be a reason."

"Trying to follow this fantastical line of thought, a logical reason would be if we shared power, it would be halved in strength. The reason would be that one of us needed to be twice as powerful," he said.

"That would be now at the end of the age," Bless said.

Rick shifted and looked uncomfortable.

"Watch this," she said, mainly to defuse the tense atmosphere, and extended her hand toward the bedside table. The teacup began to rattle and then it rose slowly about an inch off the table.

Rick got out of bed and walked over to it. He passed a hand under it, around it, then picked it up and pressed it down. It lowered back to the table easily.

"How did you do that?"

"I figured out how yesterday. Cool, huh? I lifted it with air."

"Oh."

"My psychometry is getting stronger too. It's never been useful to me before."

"Your what?"

"When I touch certain things, I get impressions of people or events associated with them. It's a fairly common ability, but it's always been weak in me. It might be something you can cultivate."

Rick crawled under the covers. "For what? The most interesting thing to do with it would be sneaking around and opening bed stand drawers to get in touch with some vibrators."

Bless looked offended.

"I'm sorry, baby. It's been a long day, and frankly, you've given me too much to think about." He closed his eyes.

She turned off her bedside lamp and tried to settle down herself. She'd almost gotten to sleep when she heard Maris scream.

22

Maris's scream reverberated through her mind, echoes of agony and terror. Bless sat bolt upright in bed.

"What's wrong?" Rick asked.

"I have to go to my sister, Maris. Something's terribly wrong."

"I'll drive you."

"No. I'll go alone," she said, pulling on a pair of jeans. "Keep an eye on Glory."

He gave a faint snort. He didn't say the words, but she heard what he was thinking as clear as water. That she wanted to keep him safe and out of the way, like a child. That he couldn't protect Glory against a demon flea.

She felt a burning pain across her neck and ran down the stairs, all her worries about Rick forced from her mind by a river of black fear for her sister.

Her keys weren't on the table by the front door where she usually left them, or in her purse. She heard a car outside the drive. She opened the door and there was Rick, pulling his car out of the garage. He backed up to the front door.

She hesitated, but ran to the car. "I couldn't find my keys."

"I figured that when I saw you rummaging around, and I got my car. Where are we going?"

"To Maris at Birch Tree. And Rick?"

"Yes?"

"Step on the gas."

He floored it. "Tell me what's going on," he said.

"Maris is in grave danger. I'm not sure of the nature." Bless could hardly get the words out. She could barely breathe. Panic hazed blood red over her eyes. Her breath came in choppy gasps.

"Are you all right?" Rick asked.

All she could do was shake her head. He started to slow down and she mouthed the word, "Go."

He went.

As quickly as it came, the curtain of panic and fear lifted, and all that was left was her dread. Rick pulled up to the dark and sleeping home, and Bless bounded from the car. Rick followed slowly. Bless rang the doorbell twice and then drew back, ready to kick in the door if no answer was forthcoming.

But a middle-aged mousy-looking woman answered the door, looking irritable. "Do you know what time it is?" she asked.

"Twenty minutes to three. I need to see my sister Maris immediately," Bless said.

"That's not possible. She's asleep. This is highly irregular," the woman said, pulling her robe close and peering around Bless to Rick.

"I need to see my sister. It's an emergency. I'm a regular visitor here and I know my rights. I demand that you let me in this instant or I'm coming in and taking her out."

"I'm going to have to call my supervisor and—"

Bless pushed her way past the woman and sprinted down the hall to Maris's room.

The woman slammed the door in Rick's face and was hot on her heels. "I'm calling the police!" she hissed, apparently afraid to yell and wake the other women up.

Bless paused outside Maris's door, trying to quell her fear at what she was going to face on the other side. She grasped white flame and entered the room. Maris's roommate was sleeping peacefully, but Maris's bed was empty. Bless moaned, her worst fears realized.

The woman clicked on the light and the blood stains on the bed stood out in stark relief against the white sheets. Bless slumped to the floor. Too late. She felt with certainty that her sister was no longer in this world. The salty taste of her tears ran into her nose and added to the metallic blood scent saturating the room.

Maris's roommate didn't move. The woman shook her and rolled her over. The roommate had been gutted. The woman's screams rent the air and Bless could hear others in the house getting up. The woman ran from the room, retching.

Bless stood, left the room, and closed the door behind her. Too late.

She walked out the front door. Rick was waiting in the car, his door open. "Was Maris all right?" he asked.

"No, she's gone. Her bed is full of blood. Her roommate is there, though; she's split down the middle, like Swank."

He jumped out of the car, alarmed. "Did you call the police?"

"No, but I'm sure the night manager will. Take me home, Rick."

"You better give a statement to the police first. They'll wonder why you showed up out of the blue. Are you sure that blood is your sister's?"

"Yes. I was too late. She wasn't supposed to die like that. I know I was supposed to save her." Guilt smothered Bless.

"You always do the best you can."

"What if the best isn't enough?" she asked in a whisper.

He took her in his arms and something broke within her. She sobbed as she never remembered doing. She sobbed out years, lifetimes, of pain until she was empty, wrung dry.

The street was full of flashing lights and cops when she raised her head.

"Ma'am? Detective Jensen says you have a statement." Bless stared into the watery blue eyes of a plainclothes officer she remembered from the emergency room.

She wiped her eyes with her hands. "Not much of one. I'm psychic and I got a strong feeling that I needed to come here tonight, that's all."

The cop looked at Rick in query and he nodded. "We were in bed and all of a sudden she had to come out to her sister's house."

"Uh, what did you think was going to happen?"

"Something bad."

He waited. "Is that it?" he finally asked.

"That's all."

His eyebrows shot up and he flipped his pad closed. "Thanks. That will be all we need."

They got in the car, the sky lightening in the east, a new day dawning.

Bless wondered how many more dawns this world would see before the end of days.

Maris shone so bright, Bless could scarcely look at her directly. She was encased in blazing white light, her form no longer definite.

"I came to see you one last time in this world," Maris said.

Bless couldn't stop the tears from flowing.

"Stop grieving," Maris said. "It did hurt like hell, pardon the pun, but not for that long. I keep telling you death is nothing to fear. The drawback is that I wanted to stay longer to support you through the coming trials. But you have all the tools to be triumphant, and most importantly, you have the strength to do so. Don't forget that Rick is your key—lean on him and don't underestimate him. Keep to your intuition and principles and you should be fine." Maris approached and embraced Bless. She was washed in peace and comfort.

"Our love will last through the ages," she said as she faded away.

"Maris!" Bless called. "Maris, please. Please don't go."

"Death is only a change of location, dear," she heard the faint whisper of Maris's voice.

With Maris and the serene aura that surrounded her gone, Bless sank to her knees, crying bitterly. She'd only gotten to know and love this sister—too late.

There was a crack of thunder. Bless heard Ginger's laughter as the blade that had cut Maris's throat solidified, dripping blood. "You cry over nothing, a retard and an idiot, a waste of space. Would you like to join her?"

"How could you? She was harmless!" Bless shrieked.

Ginger held up Maris's bloody head by her hair. "I wanted to see if I could. And I can. The circle is breaking. Don't you feel it?"

"You are filth. Inhuman filth."

Ginger looked hurt. "I was putting her out of her misery. That was no way to live. We euthanize animals with greater mercy. That's no reason to be mean to me and call me names."

"You cut off our sister's head!" Bless screamed.

Incredibly Ginger sniffed and looked as if she was going to cry.

"Why did you kill her roommate too?"

"The demons got carried away. But I know you, you're little Miss Perfect, and whenever anything goes wrong, it's always my fault." Ginger tossed Maris's head to the side. "I killed Maris myself so it would be quick and clean. You know how those demons like to drag it out."

"Nice of you."

"Thanks," Ginger said, a trembling, grateful smile on her face, Bless's sarcasm going completely over her head.

"Why don't you go ahead and get rid of the brat so everything can go back the way it used to be?" Ginger asked. "You're not thinking of my needs. These demons are poor company. I have to hide out and the food's not all that good. I'm suffering here."

"Stop consorting with them then."

"They are invested in my well-being. Unlike you," she added.

Bless snorted.

"They want the brat dead as much as I do," Ginger said.

"I don't doubt that, but I do doubt that it has anything to do with your well-being. Are you sure they wouldn't have one of their tools pull your entrails out as soon as Glory is dead?"

Ginger frowned. "Of course not."

"If you're betting your life on demons, you're both stupider and crazier than I imagined. Why do they want Glory dead? Why do you assume it has to do with you? You always believed that the world spins around you, but in this case, you need to get a grip."

A gamut of emotions played across Ginger's face—uncertainty, fear, anger, doubt. "You're jealous of me," she said. "Always have been, always will be. They told me all about you. All you want to do is to destroy me so you can have everything I have, but guess what, honey? It's never going to happen. I'm getting you first."

"You've lost what little you had of a mind. Not only do you have a loose hold on reality, you don't realize that you have absolutely nothing that I would want."

"Liar!" Ginger yelled. "Caught you in one. You like your pants on fire, don't you? That fucking is good. You're afraid I'll get that primo dick you got now. And I will, baby, count on it."

Bless shook her head. "I pity you."

"Bitch, I don't want your pity!" Ginger lunged at her with the knife that had killed Maris.

Bless woke shaking, her heart soaked with sorrow. She turned to Rick and touched his chest. He awoke instantly, a light sleeper. "Hold me," she asked.

He wrapped his arms around her and she let her sorrow break free—for her losses, the loss of the family she once had, the sisters she loved, and the life she knew. Her sobs shook her.

He held on to her tight. After a while he cried with her, his loss deep too. As her sorrow leaked out, it was replaced by gratitude that her man was man enough to anchor her pain with his own, not displace it. She loved him all the more for that.

Rick was tired of sitting on his ass doing nothing. He'd read Bless's texts, but he couldn't understand them fully. He knew he needed to back up and get a foundation. He spent the next few days in the library, most of the time on the Internet learning the basics of occultism. He was amazed at how similar the different schools of thought essentially were.

He felt the same disorientation in trying to grasp the occult as a plumber would trying to figure out how to perform a hysterectomy. A woman's works could loosely be called plumbing, but a sort most plumbers never dreamed of fixing.

He had to help Bless. After the apparent grisly death of her sister, nothing else was an option anymore. Bless kept saying that demons generally couldn't kill people physically because they weren't flesh; they had to do it indirectly, either influencing other people or using inanimate objects. But they seemed to be doing a damned good job of killing to him. And they weren't fazed by the business end of a .45. What else were his options?

Rick felt the beginning of a headache pound at his temples as he tried to focus his eyes on the computer screen. His research was frustrating.

The demons that Bless was dealing with didn't seem the sort to be fazed by folded paper demon traps or spelled chants, whether rhymed or not.

He researched exorcists, but too many came to a bad end for him to be comfortable with that method. When he read that Mother Teresa had needed an exorcism herself, possibly from getting on the wrong side of a demon when aiding someone, what hope did he have? He considered himself Christian, but he was no Mother Teresa.

His research was telling him that the only way to deal with demons effectively was through sorceries. Something about this approach made his skin crawl, but he'd crunch cockroaches and snarf snakes to save Bless. He thought about studying demonology and shuddered, a bad taste in his mouth. Snakes and roaches seemed like the same difference.

23

Rick stood in an intricately drawn chalk circle on the back porch, full of swirls and flourishes, holding up two books, one in each hand. One was a Hebrew pronunciation dictionary, the other a book of rituals of an ancient order. The Tylenol was on the steps.

His headaches were growing worse. This stuff was giving him fits. He carefully skipped over the parts about demon summoning. He didn't want to know anything about it, or his eyes to rest on the words. Frankly, even handling the books was scaring the crap out of him. But he had to be a man. He needed to find a way to fight.

It disappointed him to no end that he could find no reliable way to destroy or even send demons away. All he could find was that he could contain them. That might be enough until Bless did whatever she did to destroy them. One other thing he might be able to do was to obscure himself so they couldn't perceive him, but he didn't know if he could manage that.

The more he read, the more Bless impressed him. The mere fact that she'd warded this house well enough to keep it free of evil was amazing. She was a rare woman. In another time, she might have been labeled a prophetess or a saint. But he also knew the human side of her, the vulnerable side that he wanted to protect. The side that made him rage and want to lash out at whatever was wounding her ... *Ginger, that bitch that killed his brother.*

Rick breathed deeply and tried to clear his mind of the anger. He'd read repeatedly that the negative emotions when trying to do what he was doing could turn on him and bring upon his head exactly what he was projecting outward.

He put the books down and sat cross-legged in the circle, reaching for his Bible instead. It was the first and foremost text he'd been studying. He read that some demons needed divine assistance to be dealt with along with prayer and fasting.

It was going to be hard forgoing Bless's home-cooked meals, but if it was fasting that it was going to take, it was fasting he was going to do. According to the Bible, back in those days, demons were everywhere. According to Bless, it wasn't that there were fewer demons nowadays; it was that they merely didn't want to be perceived.

Rick swallowed hard. Praying he was already doing a-plenty.

"What do you mean you're not eating dinner? I made pork chops, fried apples, twice-backed potatoes, green bean casserole, and sweet potato pie. Aunt Praise and I can't eat all this ourselves," Bless asked Rick, frowning.

"But we can try," Praise interjected.

"I'm on a diet."

"Don't lie to me."

"Okay, okay. I'm fasting."

Praise and Bless stared at him. Praise spoke first. "For what?"

"To raise my spiritual level."

"I suggest you fast on Sundays then and grub today," Praise said. "It also wouldn't hurt if you got up and attended early Sunday services."

"You mean that one that starts at six in the morning?"

"That's the one."

Rick stifled a groan.

"I don't think your spiritual level is going to be harmed by your eating dinner," Bless said. "I've never observed any gluttony in you."

Rick's eyes closed and his nose widened. The smell emanating from the kitchen was heavenly. He'd eaten nothing the entire day.

He could feel himself weakening.

"C'mon, let's eat," Bless said, her voice warm and inviting.

He gave in, the ice chips of his resolve melting. He felt guilty when he remembered how he used to rib his cousins for not sticking to their diets. "Just push yo' fat ass away from the table," he'd tease.

They'd roll their eyes. His skinny ass had no clue what it was like. He couldn't even do it for a few hours. If Bless offered him cottage cheese, tuna fish, and a salad instead of those pork chops he smelled, he'd cuss her out.

"Baby, do you mind fixing me a plate?" he asked, knowing if he went to that stove, he'd embarrass himself and load up two or three servings.

"Sure will."

A half hour later he pushed himself away from the table, and groaned in satisfaction. "Did I tell you how good you cooked?"

"Every day," Bless said.

"Where is everybody?" He'd been too busy eating to notice the silence until now.

"Praise took Miriam shopping for clothes. They ate earlier, when you were out back. Glory is doing what she does best, sleeping."

Rick noticed her hand lying on the table, small, plump, and brown, devoid of ornament. He picked it up and kissed it. Precious, like the whole of her.

"Rick?"

"I want to put my ring on your finger. Let the world know that you're mine." He chuckled. "I guess I'm a traditionalist after all. Let's do the wedding thing, white dress, flowers, the works. I love you, baby, so let's do it right."

Bless's mouth opened, closed. Tears started flowing down her cheeks.

"What's wrong?" Rick asked, his brow furrowed in consternation. Then his heart started to pound with something like panic. Could this mean that she didn't want to marry him? He never considered—

"You never even said you loved me before!" she wailed.

He stood and drew her up in his arms. "I thought you knew, sweetheart. I thought you knew a thousand times over."

He withdrew and looked at her tearstained face. "Does—does this mean that, you don't want to?"

"No. Yes. I do, Rick, I do love you, and you know that. But—"

He kissed the trails of tears from her cheeks. "No buts. I love you, baby, more than I dreamed I could love any woman. I can't imagine being without you. I need to make you mine, stand up in front of God, my mama, and everybody and say it. You know what I mean."

She laughed through her tears and kissed him back. "I know."

"Let's go and get a ring," he said.

"It won't strain you?" she asked. "I know you're taking all this time off work."

"It's all right. Um, as long as you stay within reason."

She grinned. "I'll go get the baby."

The jeweler showed them a tray of stones. As soon as Bless saw it, she knew it was the one, a heart-shaped golden diamond. Simply mounted in gold, it would be perfect. "That's the one," she said. "I'd like it set in a simple gold band engraved on the inside with both our names, and a plain gold wedding band for you to match."

"I have some more rings to show you, some antiques," the jeweler said.

"We don't need to see anything else," Bless said.

"I insist. These are special."

He got out a large ring of keys and opened the cabinets behind him. He took out a tray encased on black velvet. He slid it in front of them and pulled the velvet away. "Feast your eyes," he said.

The rings were beautiful, baroque, with large stones of many colors, shapes, and sizes. They had a magnetic attraction to them. She touched an emerald and pearl ring encrusted with diamonds and stiffened.

A shriek went through her mind and darkness flooded her. She tried to release the ring but couldn't.

A demon peered out through the jeweler's eyes, waiting for the opening to strike. It wasn't now. Bless instantly strengthened her aura until the loathsome thing in her hand released her.

"It's a demon, Rick, get Glory out of here!" The demon's tongue was curling toward Glory like a whip. Rick took out some sort of cord and dropped it around himself and Glory, while chanting words in . . . *Hebrew?*

Bless hesitated in astonishment and the demon's tongue hit against the outside of the perimeter of where the cord was as if it were a shield.

She went to the other place, moving stealthily toward the aura of the jeweler where the demon lurked. But the demon was gone. She spun around. Glory and Rick were safe, protected by a towering light blue circle, sort of raggedy, but there.

She crossed back to her body and anxiously picked up the cord, gauging the spell.

Then she said to Rick, "This is one thing you should have left completely alone."

"Yeah, I believe you. Can we go home? I feel sick."

She took Glory from his arms and felt the shimmer of angelic wings. Glory's protectors had been out in full force. Probably all of them were needed to reinforce that raggedy circle Rick had called up. Did he realize how dangerous what he did was? How he had pulled them all into greater danger than before rather than protecting Glory? She knew he didn't. She was going to have a long talk with him and tell him the whys.

* * *

Rick asked if he could talk tomorrow and wanted to go straight up to bed. Bless went out to the enclosed back porch. Her eyes narrowed when she saw the remnants of the chalk circle he'd drawn. She walked over to examine the pile of books he'd stacked up against the wall and her heart started to pound. Lord help her. No, help him. He was a babe in esoteric matters and he had no idea of what he was getting into, the forces he could unleash, the disaster he could bring down on them all.

She knew his heart. He wanted to help her; he wanted to feel useful. But he was going to have to satisfy himself with painting the house or something, because this was simply way too deep and dangerous. They would have to have more than a long talk; they'd have to have a meeting and she might have to pull Praise in. She was going to have to think of something that could make Rick feel included—safely. If only she knew more. She still wasn't clear on the purpose of his presence related to the prophecy.

She wished Maris were here to give her advice in her dreams. She had only just gotten to know her sister, and she missed her terribly.

24

The next morning Bless played with Glory after her feeding. Time flowed without her notice as it sometimes did when she spent time with the child that she was increasingly coming to think of as hers. Miriam was in front of her children's daytime television as customary.

Aunt Praise was at work on what she called "the family story." Praise said they'd been passing things on from generation to generation by word of mouth, and it was time that someone made a written record.

Bless didn't have the heart to remind her that this was the last generation of the three. Praise knew, but conveniently decided to forget that fact.

The sun rose high in the sky before she noticed that she hadn't seen Rick yet. He always came down and had breakfast with her before he went to the library or buried himself in books.

Glory's little eyes were drooping, so she put her in her bassinet and went to their bedroom to see if he was ill. He said he didn't feel good yesterday.

He was uncharacteristically tangled up in the covers, still asleep. "Rick?" she called softly.

He didn't respond, his breaths deep and rapid. He was covered with a chill glaze of perspiration. She felt his skin, no fever, cold and clammy. Worried, she gazed at his aura for signs of illness. It seemed unchanged, but almost still, instead of the moving energy field that played around human bodies. Odd, but healthy.

She tucked the covers over him carefully and left him to his rest.

Rick writhed in his bonds. He was spread-eagled against a stone cave wall, naked, his hands and feet in shackles.

Demons surrounded him, like living stone. Ginger sat in front of him eating an apple.

She threw the core on the floor and approached him. Her eyes widened in appreciation as she took in his manhood. "That I like," she said. "But we have plenty of time for fun later. What a predicament you've gotten yourself into."

He stopped struggling; there was no point, and it was chafing his wrists and ankles raw in the too-tight shackles anyway. "What are you talking about, Ginger? Everybody has nightmares. I'll wake up from this one too."

She came closer, too close. He inhaled the scent of the Georgio perfume she wore. It was cloying and strong. He hated that scent.

She cupped his balls in her hand. The demons laughed.

He didn't like this dream one little bit.

"Do you want to hear the good part?" she whispered in his ear, her thumb caressing his penis.

"Not unless it has to do with waking up."

"Your stupidity when you cast that spell put you under my buddy's power here, and by association, my power. You left a tiny opening, a chink in the circle, and that was enough. The asshole angels wouldn't let him get to the child, but he was more than able to get to you."

She tightened her hand on his balls and he inhaled. "This means you are under my power."

"Never."

Her hand tightened yet further and he gasped. "This leaves you open for all sorts of interesting possibilities. Possession is the easiest, but too detectable and would trigger the wards. Obsession from afar is the answer, darlin'. You are my little puppet man, do you hear?"

"You're crazy. I'd die before I'd let you control me."

"That, too, all in good time."

He tried not to sigh in relief when she released the pressure from his testicles.

"Let me tell you something, Rick. Control is largely physical. I strike a reflex point, you jerk. You can't control your movement, I do. You always thought you were the shit, didn't you? You're the sucker now."

"Why don't you shut up, Ginger? You always did talk too much."

"Oh, I'll shut up. You think you're so much better than me? By the time I'm finished with you, you'll be begging for some more of this. You'll be screaming my name."

"Dream on."

She gave him a feral smile and dropped to her knees. He locked his knees against what he knew was coming next. When she took him in her mouth, he resisted, scraping his back against the stone. But her mouth was expert, sucking and applying friction until . . . release. She stood and wiped her mouth, panting slightly.

"Bless was always jealous of me and now you know why," she said triumphantly.

"You're jealous of Bless, as you should be. Because frankly, I've had a whole lot better times beating off."

Ginger screeched and slapped him openhanded across the face.

He opened his eyes with his face in the pillow, his cheek burning.

He got out of bed to go to the bathroom as he usually did, and it was with a feeling of dawning horror that he saw his chafed and bleeding wrists and ankles, and felt the raw soreness at his back. He rushed over to the full-length mirror, dropped his T-shirt on the floor, and turned to study the abrasions on his back. They were exactly as if he'd scraped his back on rock. This was impossible. Then he noticed a telltale stickiness at his groin, a residue of saliva and semen.

He started the shower. Turned the water as hot as he could take it, but he knew it wouldn't clean as deep as he wanted it to.

When he got downstairs, Bless was mopping the kitchen floor. "There you are, hon," she said. "How are you feeling? I was worried about you."

"I'm not a child," he snapped. "Why don't you lay off the worrying and do something useful like get me something to eat?" Did he say that? Rick wondered. Surely not.

Bless put the mop in the bucket. "What's wrong? Let's talk about it."

"Is it English you don't understand, woman?"

Rick was aghast. The words were coming out of his mouth, with his tongue, but he wasn't saying them. He swore he wasn't.

Bless looked at him, puzzled, with anger beginning. "All right then," she said, and turned away to the refrigerator.

His throat worked, trying to explain that the former words weren't his, but nothing came out. He tried to move to get some paper to write on, anything, but his muscles wouldn't respond. All he could do was watch her as she silently made him a ham and cheese sandwich, put potato salad on the side, and served it with a glass of orange juice. She slid the food in front of him and left the kitchen without a word. He could feel her hurt and it caused him pain.

He tried to rise from his chair to follow her and he couldn't move. He would not panic, he told himself. Just remember what Ginger said to him. She said something about obsession from afar, that he would be her puppet. She said he did this because he tried to work a spell.

He was a stupid fool. But there had to be a way out, something he could do. There simply had to be.

Bless lay across her bed, numb inside. The way Rick had spoken to her had chilled her to the core. It was uncharacteristic of him. If there was anything that Rick wasn't, it was mean. One of the things she loved best—out of the many, many things she loved about him—was his unfailing kindness.

She would have thought he wasn't feeling good, but she detected no signs of illness. Maybe the stress was getting to him, the boredom. Her mind skeetered around her deepest and most secret fear. Maybe it was her; maybe he was getting sick of her.

Was he able to leave the house? Rick got up from the table slowly, scared that he wouldn't be able to. He picked up his plate and scraped it and rinsed it off. He had no appetite after what happened.

He went and got his jacket and car keys. He made one effort to turn to Bless's room but his feet wouldn't move. Maybe he could tell Praise. He heard her moving around in the living room. No go. If he couldn't walk in there, his mouth wouldn't work to get the words out. How was it controlling him?

He walked out of the door freely to his car. He planned to go to the library, but he drove right past. Whoever or whatever was controlling him didn't think that was a good idea. He spied a sports bar, and pulled up.

"Beer, please, draft."

The bartender slid a beer toward him and he took a grateful gulp. What if he tried to make a circle of protection, and did it right this time?

Then he despaired. If he couldn't talk freely, how was he going to work spells? And it was that which got him into this mess in the first place. Apparently, his thoughts were his own. His actions were totally controlled and somehow his intentions were anticipated. How could he alert Bless to his dilemma without his awareness? That was the problem.

He ordered another beer, pressure building in his temples. Could it make him do things against his will? Like hurt Bless or the baby? He'd die first.

He remembered Ginger's voice. *That, too, all in good time,* she'd said.

She was going to toy with him and Bless like a cat with its prey before she moved in for the kill. *She's jealous of me, you know,* Ginger had said, a mad light in her eyes.

Rick had recently read of a mother who set her young children on fire and burned them alive, saying God told her to do it. There was a photo of her in the courtroom, looking confused, defiant, angry, and grief-stricken all at once.

She was found innocent by reason of insanity and institutionalized. Was she evil? Her acts were, and her children had suffered from tremendous evil. If she had some weakness that was exploited by tremendous evil, was *she* evil? If she was influenced by demons or psychotic, was she evil?

Rick didn't know. But he remembered her picture and the woman's fear and confusion and felt that somehow, somewhere, she might be forgiven. Someday her children might run to her in another world, in another life, in joyful reunion. *She knew not what she did.*

He had the same feeling about Ginger. Maybe she was a broken woman, influenced, weak, and fearful. Maybe her evil acts were an outgrowth of her mad weakness. Maybe if a person's heart was big enough, there would be room to grant her grace.

Rick motioned to the bartender to refill his beer. He knew that his heart was too human and not nearly big enough. He'd kill the bitch as soon as look at her.

25

"Aunt Praise, would you put on dinner tonight?"

"Sure, doll. You've been spoiling me. Want me to cook anything in particular?"

"Something Rick likes. I'm not hungry."

"That's a strange state of affairs. Anything wrong?"

"No, I'm okay. Thanks."

Bless wandered in front of the television and sat beside Miriam watching *Teletubbies* for a while. The giggling high-pitched voices of the characters were grating. She got up and went to lie on her bed with a novel. The words soon blurred.

What she didn't want to think about kept playing through her mind. Where was he? He'd left without a word of apology following his brusque comments, after he'd finally got out of bed. So unlike him.

Or was he showing his true colors? Bless let the book fall to the floor as she curled up on her side.

* * *

A woman with auburn hair slid onto the stool next to Rick. "I love football. I usually come here to watch it because my roommate hates it and we only have one television. Who's winning?"

He glanced at her, young, pretty, and very interested. He couldn't care less and wished she'd found another man to hit on. "Looks like the Cowboys are ahead as expected," he said.

"Aw, I always go for the underdog. Hi, my name is Cheyenne."

"I'm Rick. What are you drinking?" The words rolled off his tongue. He hadn't intended to buy her a drink.

"I'll have a beer."

A flash hit him, almost as if inserted in his mind. If he stayed with her, whatever was controlling him would have him making the two-backed beast with this lady within the hour.

He stood and slid a bill over to the bartender to cover the drinks and tips. "I have to go to the john, be back in a sec."

Thinking only of using the toilet, he walked past the men's room out the door and into his car. He felt a surge of triumph as he started the car.

Cooking smells emanated from the kitchen as Rick entered the house. Good, Bless was in there. He was determined to figure out some way to communicate to Bless what was happening to him.

But Praise was frying chicken on the stove. "Hi, Rick," she said without turning around, unnerving him.

"Where's Glory?" He'd meant to ask where Bless was.

"Either with Bless or asleep in her crib. Why?"

Fear as he'd never felt filled him as he crept toward Glory's room. He tried to stop, to the point of grabbing and holding something. But he couldn't. His body wasn't his own. If he could have screamed, fallen, anything, he would have.

He stood in the doorway of Glory's nursery and approached her, his hands outstretched and reaching for her tiny neck—and ran into a wall of what felt like rushing, silent air. He could approach her no closer. He wanted to cry with relief. Her protectors were on the job

"Thank you, Lord!" he said fervently. A white-hot pain ran down his spine. He bit back a scream as he sank to the floor in agony.

He lay there a few seconds, breathing hard. Then he struggled to his feet to find Bless.

She was lying on the bed, asleep. He eased down beside her, wanting to kiss her awake. He bent over her tenderly, to brush her lips with his own. And then yelled in her ear, "So this is what your lazy behind does all day? Sleep? No wonder you're so fat."

Was that a heart attack he was having? He'd never spoken to a woman like that in his life, much less yelled in her ear when she was sleeping. His mama would have got a belt and whipped his ass; she wouldn't have cared how old or big he was. Surely Bless could read the horror in his eyes.

Bless's eyes opened and gazed into his own. "What is wrong with you?" she asked.

"Hell," he said, relieved he could say that at least. Would she understand the inference? But what followed was terrible. "When are you going back to work? Praise watches the kid. You're just lazing around, getting fatter. I'm getting sick of looking at you."

With those words, he left the room.

* * *

She wouldn't cry, she wouldn't cry, Bless repeated to herself as if it were a mantra. What was happening? Why did he change all of a sudden? No wards were ringing, there was no warning of a supernatural attacker, yet Rick's personality had changed radically.

Or had it? Maybe he was only putting up a front. But for what? Worse, maybe now that he'd gotten to know her really well . . . maybe he didn't like her that much anymore. Men had never liked her in that way before, like a woman. He was her very first . . . real lover, as in lover who made her feel wholly loved. Was that already past tense?

She wouldn't cry.

Bless stood, raised her chin, and went to the kitchen to eat supper.

He was already eating. "Wonderful fried chicken, Praise. And your biscuits are so fluffy. I swear your food melts in my mouth."

Aunt Praise beamed at him. "Let me get you some more. More ice tea?"

"Please."

He didn't even look at Bless. What was happening?

"Get a plate, Bless," Aunt Praise said.

"I'm not hungry."

"Nonsense. Let me fix you up a plate."

"Leave her be if she doesn't want to eat," Rick said. "Maybe she's starting a diet."

Bless turned a baleful gaze on him. "We need to talk."

"Sure, about what?" he said cheerfully around a drumstick.

She never so much wanted to slap a man silly in her life.

"First, we need to talk about what happened in the jewelry store, and then I can think of a few other matters to add to that."

"What happened in the jewelry store?" Praise asked, sitting at the table with a cup of coffee.

"A demon attacked us, and Rick attempted a spell."

"What? Spell casting when demons are around, and they always are, is extremely dangerous," Praise said, frowning.

"Spell casting is something I don't do," Bless said. "No matter what the intent, no matter if they're labeled white magic or such. These sorts of things have too much propensity to be gateways for uncleanliness. I don't foretell the future or do readings. I never do rituals, spells, or charms. I was wrong to call up Malik, and it is something I generally never do—call up spirits of any sort. Praise disagrees with me and she's allowed to have her own opinions in the matter. But in my opinion, such things are not of the light."

"I'm not quite as pure as Bless, and don't see the harm in a touch of dabbling. But with all that's going on, it would be foolhardy to do those things Bless listed. You need to steer clear. We can hone your senses, so maybe you can perceive more and gain understanding that way. But leave the easy path of spells and chants alone. You end up in dire straits. We're essentially under siege."

They both looked at Rick expectantly for his response.

"Are you two done lecturing me? If so, I'd sure love a piece of that peach cobbler with ice cream."

After he got it, he took his cobbler and went to the couch in the sewing room and turned the television on in there.

Bless cleaned the kitchen while Aunt Praise fed Glory. "I never did get around to telling you what happened at that jewelry store," Bless said.

Praise raised her head. Glory was busy greedily sucking the bottle. "Go ahead."

"Rick was going to buy me an engagement ring."

Praise squealed. "Oh, Bless! I'm so happy for you. I knew it was coming. You deserve it, honey, and he's such a good man."

"I dunno," she mumbled.

"What do you mean?"

"Today had been awful. He's been saying all this crazy mean stuff, calling me fat . . ." Her voice went husky with hurt. "He said he was sick of looking at me."

Praise waved her hand. "Once men actually make that big commitment step, they get scared. They always do something terrible to drive you away. Just stick it through, it will pass. I hear all women have to go through some variation of premarital jitters from men."

"But he's so different. And he's not said another word about the engagement ring."

"Give him time, dear. You say he's been acting strange for one day, but in all the days you've known him before, he's been his usual loving self, right?"

"Well, right."

"Sounds like you're having premarital jitters, too."

"Maybe so, Aunt Praise."

The phone rang and Bless reached over to pick it up. A sultry feminine voice asked, "Is Rick there?"

"Yes, may I tell him who's calling?"

"Oh, yeah. Tell him this is Cheyenne, from the bar."

26

Bless's hand tightened on the phone. Cheyenne from the bar? "Okay," she said, dragging the word out. "Let me go and get him."

She walked to the sewing room. This she hadn't expected. Nope, not at all. He was stretched out on the sofa, his eyes on the television.

"Cheyenne from the bar is on the phone."

He looked up at her, his mouth stretched out in a grin. "Really? Good." He reached over and picked up the extension. "Hey, baby. Yeah. Nothing. To-night? That sounds good. Where are you? No, I'll remember. Give me twenty minutes. Me too. Bye."

He put the phone on the cradle and bounded up. "I'm going out."

"You've got to be kidding," Bless said.

"What are you jabbering about now?"

"You aren't going to disrespect me in front of my face, in my own house, by going out with some slut you met in a bar." Her voice was rising, becoming as uncontrolled as her emotions.

"You're absolutely right. I'm not going to do it in front of your face in your house at all."

He whistled a merry tune as he went and scooped up his car keys and jacket. The door slammed behind him.

Bless was beside herself. She hurried back to the kitchen. She paced in front of Praise, her mouth moving, but no words were coming out.

"Calm down, child, and collect yourself," Praise said. "What is the matter?"

"He went out with that woman. He taunted me and went out to see her tonight."

"You're joking."

Bless wiped her eyes. "I don't know what to do. I see this stuff on television, read it in books, but in my life—I've never come close."

"You could follow him," Praise suggested.

"For what? What is the worst he can do? Screw her? Would that make me feel worse than I do now?" She sank into a chair. "Not really. What if they sit in the old folks home and play canasta? That wouldn't make me feel much better either. He threw it in my face. He didn't care how I felt. It was—so cruel."

As if on cue, Glory started to cry. Both of them started, unused to her wail. She was a placid baby.

"My jangled energy fields must have upset her."

"I have some chocolate silk pie in the freezer, premium stuff. Here, hold Glory and let me get you a piece," Praise said.

A few minutes later, with the dark creamy chocolate melting in her mouth and sliding down her throat, Bless started to calm down. Praise knew what to do.

"I'm not going to marry him," Bless announced.

"This is an evil day. I need to do a casting," Praise murmured.

"No! I can't believe you'd consider bringing spirit influence into this house. You don't know what you'd be dragging in."

"Have you considered that Rick could be charmed?"

"I could tell. His aura is unchanged. There is no difference in the atmosphere around him."

"There are subtleties upon subtleties," Praise said.

Bless stared at the smears of chocolate on her plate. It was no spell that had Rick in its grasp. It was only her worst fear coming true. The one where he realized that she wasn't good enough for him after all.

"You thought an ugly cow like you could have a man?" Ginger whispered in her ear. "See what you get when you cross over in my territory, fat heifer?"

It was a cave. Ginger was surrounded by demons in the guise of naked, well-developed men.

"What is it to you?" Bless's eyes narrowed with suspicion. "What do you have to do with it?"

"I don't have a damned thing to do with your inadequacies. I heard that your boyfriend is out with a hottie. You know how closely you all are observed. Wanna see?"

"No."

But a demon waved its hand and a cave wall shimmered. What looked like Rick's buttocks were pumping up and down over a slim white woman, her blond hair spread over the pillow. The image faded after a couple of seconds.

What was interesting was that it didn't hurt

nearly as much as when he walked out on her the way he did.

"Not so hot shit now, are you? I bet you're pretty mad. Want to do some demon slaying? But your powers don't work in your dreams, do you notice?"

"I've noticed. Are you done? All this is probably cutting into my theta sleep and I need my rest."

Tremors shook Ginger's hand as she pointed a finger at Bless, her face twisted in a grimace. "My entire life you have always been the good one, the better one, the best sister. I had this one thing over you. I was the fuckable one. That one thing and you try to take it. You have nerve. You, you—"

"Ginger."

Ginger lowered her hand. "What?"

"They have medication available for your problem. I can get you a referral to a good shrink—"

Ginger shrieked.

"Guess you didn't like that idea. But honey, look at yourself. You're like somebody who doesn't have a clue how to swim stuck in the middle of the deep end." Bless nodded sagely. "You need help."

Ginger tried to strike her, but her hands went right through her. She struck at her again and again, her hands striking air, her shrieks reverberating until Bless covered her noncorporeal ears.

She studied her sister, shaking her head. Despite all Ginger was putting her through and what she was going through personally, she pitied her sister, the poor crazy thing.

Rick drove a few miles, then the compulsion to go to the woman's house faded. He pulled over and leaned his hot head against the steering wheel.

Now it was time to panic. He couldn't believe

what he'd said and done to Bless. She'd stood there, filling with pain, and hadn't suspected for a second what was really happening. How could she believe that he'd say those things to her? That he'd propose marriage one day and go out the next day with some bimbo he'd met at a bar?

Didn't she know him better than that?

He started the car, intending to go back home. He couldn't turn on the crossroad he needed to get to the house. Frustrated, he pulled over. He was going to have to go to Atlanta before he did something irreversibly harmful, but how? If whatever was binding him wouldn't let him turn the damn corner, it wasn't going to let him drive the stretch of highway it would take to get free of Red Creek.

He'd never felt so helpless, a prisoner in his own body. "Malik?" he called.

The pain he felt in Glory's room when he thanked God for protecting him stung him in retaliation. Good, it wasn't expecting that. He called his brother without much conscious thought, letting it slip out.

He waited, but no ghostly Malik materialized to help him out of this jam. But somehow he felt his brother was near, and that thought comforted him a little.

Rick leaned his head back on the seat and closed his eyes. The only places he could go—bars, clubs, the homes of strange women—would lead to disaster, and he couldn't return to Bless. His alternative was to stay put.

He wondered what the limits of this thing's ability were.

Although it discerned his intentions and controlled his nerves and muscles to an extent, it made him say things only when he was going to talk anyway. Well, it was going to have to get real good at controlling him, because he wasn't going to do a damn thing. He could sit here and rot in this car for all he cared right now.

Sometime later he opened his eyes to tapping at the window. A policeman was shining his flashlight in at him. "Having trouble, son?" the man asked.

Son? That was one step up from boy. He was way too old to be this man's son. Rick considered flashing his badge, then reconsidered. "No, I'm waiting for someone."

"You've been here quite a while."

"Maybe they've stood me up. I'd like to wait a little longer though."

The cop frowned. "I think you should move along, boy." *Boy?* Oh, no. He pulled out his badge. "Detective Richard Jenson, Atlanta. I don't believe I'm your son or your boy. I'm well within my rights waiting here. Now, if you'd move along."

The cop turned red and started to sputter. Rick raised an eyebrow. Finally the policeman wheeled and marched back to his car without a word.

Rick sighed and drummed his fingers against the dashboard. If getting locked up wouldn't have posed serious problems to his job back home, he'd have considered it as a convenient way to take himself out of the picture, at least for a while. That good ol' Southern cop would have been more than happy to oblige.

He leaned the seat back and closed his eyes. He hoped he wouldn't dream.

27

Bless woke up at two in the morning after her encounter with Ginger. Rick wasn't in the bed, wasn't in the house. She tried to get back to sleep, but it was hopeless. Her insides were stretched out tighter than an overstuffed sausage. Finally she got up and went to the kitchen.

She was finishing the rest of that chocolate silk pie when she heard Rick let himself in. Now it was three-thirty, the pie tin was empty, Bless was back in bed, and he was moving around downstairs. Her heart pounded as she heard him make his way up to the bedroom. She'd never had the opportunity for much confrontation before, but she discovered she didn't relish it.

Rick walked in and she was shocked at his face. He looked weary, grieved, lines grooved where there had been none a few days before. It was like he'd aged a decade overnight. His shoulders were bowed as if under a great weight. He started un-buckling his belt without saying hello, how are you, or even kiss my ass.

Suddenly all the self-loathing, all the trepidation and fear of losing him, was replaced by sheer fury. Her fingers clenched and she swung her feet over the edge of the bed. "How dare you come waltzing into my bedroom at almost four in the morning?"

"Hey, I'm tired. Can we continue the drama in the morning?"

"Oh, hell no. You been out with some woman and you don't even have a lie for me to retain my dignity?" Bless breathed hard.

"Now you want me to lie to you. You women can't make up your minds."

Red haze rose in front of her eyes and she picked up the closest lamp, ripped the cord out of the wall, and threw it at him. He ducked and it crashed against the wall, shattering.

"You're going to wake up the brat," he said.

"Get out of my house," Bless screamed. "Get your crap together, pack your bags, and get the fu—"

"What's going on in here?" Praise asked, sticking her head in the door.

"He's getting out." Bless sank on the bed and buried her face in her hands. She wasn't going to cry in front of this SOB if it killed her.

She looked up at Rick and Praise staring at her. "You still here?" she asked him. "Something wrong with your hearing?"

"Look, Bless," Praise whispered and pointed.

Rick was clutching a shard of the broken lamp so hard in his left hand that the blood was running down his fingers. He wasn't letting go, but was squeezing harder.

"What's wrong with you?" she asked.

"Nothing, bitch. You're the one screaming and yelling," he said with a shrug.

Yet he didn't let up the pressure a bit, and blood started to drip on the carpet. He'd called Glory a brat. He'd never referred to her that way. That was what Ginger called the baby.

"He's under a spell," Bless whispered.

Praise stared at his hand gripping the sharp cutting edges hard and purposefully as he stood there in a casual and belligerent matter. "I think that's a strong possibility," she said.

Suddenly Rick released the fragment and sprinted out of the room.

"Stop!" Bless cried and tried to catch him, but there was no hope. He grabbed his car keys and ran out the front door before she barely cleared the bedroom.

He was gone.

Stop running, stop running, stop running, he begged his body. He tried to apply every iota of will he had to stop his forward momentum. They'd figured it out. Bless would be able to free him, he knew it.

Apparently Ginger and her cohorts knew it too, because as soon as he was discovered, he was forced to bolt. He was flying down the highway now, with no idea of his destination. He assumed he was going to her.

His cut and bleeding hand grasped the steering wheel as if it were Ginger's neck.

Bless sank to the floor in the foyer, the front door open, watching Rick speed away. The tension and strain of the past day snapped within her and she sobbed.

Aunt Praise closed the front door, locked it, and handed her a box of tissues. Bless wailed her sadness and the anger that she'd held inside, and now, her fear for the man she loved. Being able to cry your heart out was one of the nicer things about being a woman.

She felt a lot better when she was done, ready to tackle the problem at hand.

"Coffee?" Aunt Praise asked.

"That's exactly what I need." The problem at hand was finding Rick. She followed her aunt to the kitchen. "Do you think we can break the spell from afar?"

Praise sucked her teeth. "For that type of thing you usually need the person's presence."

"If I find Ginger, I'll find him."

Aunt Praise nodded. "That's what I was thinking."

Bless grew still, hardly able to breathe. "What if she kills him?"

"I don't think she will. She knows that he's the best hold over you she's got. She wants the baby. And she wants to hurt you."

"I have visitations. She's mad, stone-cold crazy. But it still hurts, how much she hates me. I'm her sister. What did I ever do to her?"

Praise poured two mugs of coffee. She set one in front of Bless. "You're a better person than her. Always have been, always will be, and she knows it. She's always tried to cut you down, shrivel your self-esteem. I've observed you two all your lives."

"Was our mother like that also? Why do they go always go crazy?"

Praise sipped her coffee. "Your mother was somewhat like that, a reflection but not a carbon copy. I think they go crazy because of a chemical imbalance in the brain. But this imbalance reflects the soul. I think as the circle turns and time passes, it grows worse with the generations. We're not meant to recycle our souls like this."

"So the second sister's inherent mental imbalance grows worse, as does the third's developmental disability. But what about my power?"

"It grows stronger. You do things that I can't dream about."

Bless stared into the distance. "I need to bring everything I've got to hunt for Rick. I'm going to have to leave Red Creek, and I'm not going to be able to take Glory with me."

"I know."

"Praise, you know what I'm entrusting you with."

Her lips thinned. "The future."

That was right, the future of the family, and maybe the very future of humankind.

"You can trust me, Bless. I killed and I need to balance that karma. At the time I thought there was no other choice to save you girls . . . But the universe always provides another choice. I simply didn't perceive it."

"Your guard has to be up at all times. The house has to be clean and shielded, the energies balanced. The wards have to be charged properly."

"I can do that," Praise said.

"This is the most important thing. I need to instruct you on how to battle demons. Miriam can help you."

"Miriam!"

"I didn't tell you about Miriam and Maris? I could have sworn I did. Things have been so hectic."

"Tell me what about Maris and Miriam?"

"They don't really live in this world. They live on another plane, a beautiful place. Maris trained me. She says Miriam is like her, but only not at the same place. Apparently we can't communicate across generations. Miriam can't contact me, but she can contact you, if there is willingness. You know what else she said that freaked me out? We are the same soul, you and me, Miriam and her. Isn't that a trip?"

Praise looked at her as if she'd lost her mind. "What are you talking about?"

"Listen up while I tell you how to kill a demon. And I bet Miriam comes in your dreams to complete your training. Time is different there. Days might pass. I also advise you to take a couple of ibuprofen before you lay down."

"But I don't want to slay demons. It's not my thing. You seem to have a knack for it, though."

"I don't think you'll actually ever have to slay a demon, Aunt Praise. But I want you to know what to do in a worst-case scenario if I'm not here. I need you to do this."

Praise took a few sips of coffee, clearly wanting to say no, but seeing the need to say yes. "I guess so, child. You're going to be the death of me."

"I hope not," Bless said. She rose from the table. "I'm going to go back to bed. I need to get some sleep. I plan to set out by nightfall."

"Nightfall! It's a dangerous time to travel."

"It's a good time to search for demons. It's when they're most active."

Bless gave Praise a little instruction on demon battle and how to move between the planes, before she went back to her room. Residues of discord still snaked lazily around the room. Bless cleansed it with white light and extended the light to every nook and corner of the house to ensure there wasn't a dust mote of evil lurking.

A pain hit her in her heart that doubled her over. She straightened slowly. She was worrying about everything but the one thing that was hurting her most. What was going to happen to Rick? She had to find him. Failure was not an option.

When he was nasty to her the past couple of days, it was as if he'd turned into a stranger. If that had continued, she could have let him go, because that man wasn't the Rick she loved. But without her Rick, kind, tender, funny—it would be painful living without him in the world.

She spread her arms and threw her head back, pulling the power in. She stretched and let a wave of power emanate from her being as she repeatedly chanted the words she always said when she evoked power. *Lord, grant me your grace, along with the power and the strength as your will and not mine be done.*

The walls rippled with the intensity of the energies. The breadth and depth of her power stunned her. She fell to her knees, reeling under it.

Moments later, Bless raised her head, her eyes blazing, a small smile curving her lips.

Demons, get ready. This slayer is going to open a can of whup-ass on you.

28

Bless pulled to the shoulder of the dark Georgia country road and climbed over a barbed wire fence that enclosed a harvested hay field, its mounds of straw seeming like still goblins crouching in the night.

She needed to find the location of Ginger and Rick, and she needed open air and lots of it to do that.

She stood in the black field under glittering stars in the silver half-moon light, spread her arms, and drew energies from the air. She rocked a little with the scope of her newfound power and raised a clear crystal to the sky, channeling her power into it. A thin beam of light streamed to the west.

She stayed for a while, first trying to locate Ginger, and then searching longer for the shape of her beloved's soul in the winds. Nothing. Bless got back in her car and drove west, trying not to feel upset that she couldn't sense Rick. If she followed the crystal, it would lead her to where she needed to go.

* * *

In late fall, the riotous color that blanketed the Missouri hills was fading, and the trees were showing their bones. Rick slammed the door to his vehicle. His chest tightened. He wasn't a bit psychic, yet he could sense the evil here. He moved into the dark hole that was the entrance of the cave.

Ginger was waiting for him in there. He knew that. His flesh crawled with the memory of his dream. It was so black that he couldn't see his hand in front of his face, yet his body moved forward confidently. He didn't have far to walk.

She sat on a bed of leaves on the floor of the cave, and despite the blackness, she appeared to be reading a book. She raised her head as he entered. The hairs on his arms stood up, and he could feel goose bumps forming. He was somehow able to see her clearly, although there were presences here that he couldn't see. He swallowed hard as he weighed the odds against his leaving this cave alive.

Ginger set the book down and stood. "You failed me. Name me a reason why I shouldn't have one of my demon friends here immobilize you while I kill you like Swank? They like me to take your dick off first and use it as a gag. Although after that's done, a gag is hardly necessary. Usually a man's vocal cords are about worn clean down from screaming."

He remembered what he told Bless a while back. He really didn't believe it himself, but it sounded good. Death is only a change of location. He and Bless could never be separated. One way or another they'd always end up together again. One life or another. He visualized Bless. She was smiling up at him, leaning against him. What she didn't know was that she was also holding him up. Because of who she was, she brought him to a higher standard, a better place. She was telling him that he would get through this.

"You're not listening to me!" Ginger yelled. "Make him pay attention to me."

"They can't." Rick looked her in the eyes and shook his head. "They want to make like they're gods or something, but they can't even control our minds or know our thoughts. How can you be a god and not know thoughts? Folks pray to their gods!"

There was a crazy light in Ginger's eyes. She didn't seem to be possessed as she was in his home; close up she just seemed crazy.

Her robe dropped to the floor and she stood in front of him naked. She struck a pose. Then she shifted and posed again, preening. Now he knew she was crazy. She looked absolutely ridiculous.

She put her hands on her hips and thrust her breasts out and in like a chicken. "Even though you failed me, I could use a little companionship. Guess what?" she asked, all perky, like he'd won the prize sweepstakes. "You get to fuck me now."

With his body under outside control, he had no choice but to go through the motions, but apparently even demonic spells couldn't extend to summoning up an erection on demand. Ginger didn't do it for him; she really didn't.

He was so turned off, even friction didn't work. Right now she was sucking on his joint like it was a dime store lollipop and she was a fat kid. Quite uncomfortable. It wasn't nearly as uncomfortable as those demons could make him, so he should thank the Lord for small mercies.

She raised her head and reached up and slapped

him so hard his ears rang. "Get hard, motherfucker," she screamed.

She thought that was going to work? This girl wasn't too bright. She stepped away from him and kicked him, then turned and paced the cave, talking to her unseen colleagues.

"I know he can still be useful." She paced faster. "All right!" she yelled. "Bind him further so he can't speak."

His tongue turned to lead in his mouth. He opened his mouth and tried to speak but no sound issued. His spirits lifted. This meant they had other plans in mind and weren't going to kill him, at least not yet.

Bless drove west, stopping in bigger cities twice to shop for weapons she might need. She picked up several knives and strap-on holsters to hold them, and purchased a few more crystals, some vials of scented oils, and candles.

She periodically took a two- or three-hour nap, whenever the road started blurring in front of her, and she stopped to fill up her gas tank or buy some food at a rest stop or convenience store. Outside of those things, she drove on west following the crystal's light.

When she crossed the Missouri state line, she shivered, although the car was well heated. She was drawing closer.

Several hours later, right when the sun dropped below the horizon, the light of the crystal pointed off the dirt road into the wilderness. She closed her eyes, steadied her breathing, and tried to *feel* what she should do.

She should go into those woods. Bless strapped

on the knives and packed her backpack, including a two-liter bottle of water. She had no idea how long she'd need to walk.

The crystal glowed and lit her path through the brush and trees. She used power to dissipate her fatigue and send it into the earth. The sky turned black and one by one the stars pierced the night with their cold light. Night sounds started to fill the air. Somewhere close a coyote howled.

Bless halted, then the crystal's light had her turn to the left, through a dense stand of trees. If she sent power out, whoever, whatever was out there would be warned of her arrival. Something told her that stealth would be healthier. She struggled through the trees, coming upon a stream on the other side. The crystal's light shone straight out, over the stream. She'd have to cross it.

It was too cold to hike in wet pants, so she took them off, folded them, and put them in her backpack along with her socks and sneakers. She moved into the frigid running water. She was thankful that it was only about three feet deep in the middle.

As soon as she set foot on dry land, she gasped, gathered power, and peered into the dark shadows while dressing as fast as she could. The evil hung in the air and saturated the earth. She glanced backward. Clear running water cleanses evil, so that was why she hadn't sensed it while crossing the stream.

Demons ahead, many of them. Bless lifted her chin. She walked on, wrapped in power, prepared to battle and prepared to die.

Suddenly the crystal's beam moved downward, pointing into the earth. She was supposed to go underground? That wasn't something she was enthused about doing. But she pulled away the brush from the spot where the crystal's light fell and saw a black hole gaping in the ground. She lifted the crystal and it shone steadily into the hole. She was supposed to go in there. The hole was barely wider than she was.

She dropped a rock down first. She heard nothing. Great, wonderful, she thought as she crouched down and swung her legs into the hole. She stuck the crystal between her breasts. Power shimmered almost visibly around her, dampening the vibrations of her aura as she eased her body down into the black earth.

It was claustrophobic, a narrow tunnel down, until her foot struck rock. She dropped against what felt like a rock wall. She took the crystal out and held it up.

As the light flared forth, her heart sank. She was on a ledge in the middle of a rock wall with shelves and outcroppings, at what looked like a good fifty feet from the floor of the cave. Rock climbing had never been on any list of her favorite activities. She was a nurse who liked to sew, read, and cook. Things were becoming way more physical than she preferred.

Her eyes mapped out a way she'd be able to grip the ledges with her hands and feet on the way down. She tucked the crystal back in, plunging herself back into darkness. She didn't need to see to be tempted to look down, but this she would have to do by power, feel, and faith.

As she descended, her body pressed into the wall. She almost felt the ancient cave's pulse, humming with power from the bowels of the earth. The earth was intimately human, her body made from the same substance, and to it her body would return.

Bless had an idea. The demons would not be able to discern the ripple of earth power. They were not of earth, but of air and fire. She infused the walls of the cave with her essence, her power, and felt it spread. The cave responded as if she were its child, infusing her with its power as she labored.

She sent forth a thought form of Rick—where was he? It raced through the stone walls of the caverns. The cave was silent in reply. It did not recognize him within. Her feet finally touched the cave floor. Rick not here? She took out her crystal and it glowed clear, leading the way. He had to be.

29

The crystal led her to a cramped tunnel. She sensed an expansive cavern at the tunnel's exit. A pitch-back cavern filled with demons. She tucked the crystal between her breasts to hide its light and crossed into that other place. To her surprise, the crystal still felt solid against her skin as did her knife holsters and backpack. When she crossed, she took images of whatever material objects she had on her person such as clothes, but they were as insubstantial as she was in that other place.

She took out the crystal and the light shone steady in her hand, still pointing the way forward. She unsheathed the knife, sharp and material, an astral knife, well suited to cut demon flesh. She reached out toward the stone and her hand sank through it. She pulled her hand back and willed materiality, then touched the cold, hard rock. She'd been gifted with another power. She could choose to be flesh in this place.

She resheathed the knife and tucked the crystal away, dampening her aura down enough so that she could slip in among them and start the slaughter unnoticed. At least that was her plan.

There were about a dozen of them. Their auras were all muddy red, the color of rotten blood. She could discern their movements, shapes, and sizes by their auras in the darkness. They were eating what looked like flesh, fighting, copulating, their bodies writhing in a parody of pleasure. The room was palpable with fear, and pain, greed and death, all the things demons glory in. This must be their break area.

She didn't know how she knew how to kill demons when they were in the flesh; she simply did. They were tougher than humans, somewhat harder to kill. But they died easily enough. The best place was the eyes. Then they went quickly with no time to scream.

She unsheathed her knife and stabbed the closest one, who was gnawing on what looked like a human arm, through its eye in the center of its forehead. It went down without a whimper, black demon gore pouring on the floor. She launched herself through the air and moved quickly to two of them copulating doggy style. She stabbed the top one first, a lizardy one, who grunted and relaxed. The spider one screeched, probably pissed that it didn't get its goodies, and lashed out at the lizard with its back legs. Bless spun away and leaped up soundlessly, burying the knife in the center of the cluster of demon eyes. She rolled off the dead demon spider and stabbed a demon with eyes in the back of its head that was masturbating with one hand and eating raw flesh with another. Since it had four hands, she supposed it was used to multitasking.

By then, Bless was covered with black stinking demon blood and the slaughter was getting some attention. A cacophony of howls and screams filled the air and the cavern suddenly glowed with yellowish light. Oops, there went her cover. Every monster's eyes turned to her and there was a charge.

She leaped up and hovered in midair over the demons. Two winged demons rose to meet her, shooting red lances of venomous power.

Power sang within her. She motioned toward them, barely focusing her intentions, and they both exploded to ash.

"You call yourselves demons? Maybe some fairies wandered into this cave and got lost?" she mocked them.

There was a unified scream of fury. Demons of that sort had absolutely no tolerance for criticism and even less of a sense of humor.

Bless descended. The power arcing toward her was as if the cavern had exploded with fireworks. She met it with a clear mirror of magic that deflected the energies and returned them. The remaining demons burst into flames.

Bless rejoined her body and rushed to leave before demon reinforcements came, probably a more powerful class that would be more time-consuming to vanquish. She had to find Rick.

The crystal led the way. She felt the ripple of magic ahead. Tucking her crystal away, she drew power from the ancient cavern. The light grew and she almost had to cover her eyes. She quailed for a moment and dampened her aura into the rock of the cave. A fallen angel. How could she prevail?

How can you not? a voice said in her mind. She felt better, her power from a far greater source than any fallen one, bound in darkness.

"Please, come forth. I have no desire to harm you. You should calm down and we can talk." The light coalesced into a stunningly handsome man with hair flowing over his shoulders like gold. His voice was calm and quiet, his words reasonable. She gazed at his body. She'd never seen the like before. He was wearing nothing but ripped jeans that exposed the muscles of his thighs. He must have been six-foot-six, all lean, cut muscle with the chiseled features of, well, an angel. She noted the overgenerous bulge in his pants.

An angel of lust. He radiated raw sexual energy of an intensity she'd never imagined. But he said he had no desire to harm her, an obvious lie. And his looks were nothing but deception and illusion.

"Come here," he said, his hand dropping below his waist and his bulge perceptibly thickening. "Let's . . . talk."

"Oh, give it a break," Bless said, and sent a blast of silver flame in answer.

He replied with a lightning bolt and it was on.

Bless was barely holding her own, maintaining her shields so as not to be blasted to ash. She didn't see how she was going to defeat him. Even with her increased power, he was simply too much for her. What was she going to do?

Bless responded as was her habit when she hit an obstacle that caused her despair. She surrendered, not to the problem, but to the Lord. She dropped to her knees and lowered her eyes in prayer.

A red glow started around the fallen angel's feet. He didn't notice it at first, bent on sending blasts of destruction toward her. Tiny flames licked at him. He looked down in alarm and tried to rise, but the rock of the floor had softened. The red glow intensified to an inferno and the demon screamed. He was sinking.

Bless continued with prayers of gratitude as he sank downward out of sight, screaming in agony as hell took him.

The ground sealed, the red glow faded, and Bless's way was clear. She spied a light up ahead. The beam of the crystal sped to it. She moved quickly toward the light, no more demons accosting her.

Bless peeked into the lighted cavern.

"C'mon in, sis. Took you long enough to get here," Ginger said with a cheerful grin.

Bless walked in. She looked around, but there were no demons in sight. She pulled the knife from her shoulder holster nevertheless, which more than anything else was a message to Ginger that she wasn't playing around. "Where's Rick?"

"You just missed him."

Bless was at Ginger's side in a flash, her knife at her sister's neck. "Where's Rick?" she repeated.

"I didn't think that a person of your weight could move that fast. Why don't you sit your fat ass down? You're not going to kill me. You don't have the balls. Figuratively speaking."

"I don't have to kill you, Ginger. Scarring that pretty face of yours would work even better, don't you think?" Bless pressed the edge of the knife into Ginger's cheek.

Demons popped in, grinning. Ginger's eyes rolled wildly. "I spared his life, and sent him away before the demons got to him. I'm going to tell you where he is. Let me go!"

"Tell me now. If he's dead, your face is going to resemble hamburger."

Pain streaked through Bless as she said the words, *If he's dead*. She didn't know if she could bear it. A tiny trickle of blood ran down Ginger's cheek.

Ginger screamed. "He's alive! I swear. He just left!" She threw out her arms to the demons. "Help me, damnit."

Bless gave a baleful glance at the demons and they drew back.

"Cowardly fuckers," Ginger muttered.

Not moving the knife, Bless took out the crystal and raised it. The beam of light flared out to the north. He was alive. She wheeled and ran, following the beam of light, ignoring Ginger's screeches and the cackles of the demons.

30

Rick didn't know if what was driving him was a demon or a man, but at this point he didn't care too much. Despite his attempts to be stoic and philosophize, he was glad to be alive.

The hulk that drove him had the shape and flesh of a man, but the whites of his eyes were red, as if they'd been dipped in blood. Most unnerving. Rick had nicknamed him Igor.

Rick had spent most of the drive looking out the window. That was one thing he could still do, see. He supposed he should be thankful for that.

He couldn't talk and couldn't hear. The quiet was the strangest thing of all. He never realized how accustomed he was to small sounds. The worst thing was that he couldn't walk. He could stand and bear weight, but the muscles that propelled him forward refused to work.

They entered Saint Louis. He'd always liked the city. It had some flavor to it, unlike some sterile modern metropolises. His driver sped to the inner city with its crumbling brick town houses and characteristic blight. The car slowed down. Rick looked at Igor quizzically. Where were they going? He swallowed as he contemplated the unpleasant purposes why he could have been kept alive.

He didn't have long to wonder. Igor reached over him, opened the passenger door, and kicked him out of the car. Rick hit the concrete hard and everything went black.

Bless headed north up the highway, her heart pounding. She sensed Rick was close. If the crystal had led her to the caverns, she must have just missed him as Ginger said.

Her eyes burned with fatigue. The sun was peeking over the horizon from the east, the sky a riot of morning pink, blue, and orange.

She hoped the coming day would bring her joy, and that meant she would find Rick and break the spell that bound him. Her mind replayed everything she knew about obsessions and spell breaking over the generations. She could perform a ritual to dispel it, or she could lean on faith. Bless would keep to her path and principles, and that meant using faith, a much more passive thing, a surrendering. It was difficult not to take action when something meant this much.

There still was the achy pit in the bottom of her belly from where Rick had wounded her so. It was her weakness, a vulnerability she couldn't afford. For anybody to be able to hurt you to the quick with their words, there had to be a place within where you believed them.

There was a place within where she still believed

she was ugly, where she still felt unworthy of Rick's love. A place that could be a gateway and that sorely needed healing.

She breathed in and out slow and deep. Bless contemplated herself, who she was, her flaws, her strengths. Did she like this person? She wasn't too bad, considering. She had the qualities she valued in others. The things that she was beating herself up for weren't important down deep. The body was merely a tool, meat, and hers was healthy and gave and received pleasure. What more mattered? Her soul blazed like the sun. And with this knowing came acceptance.

The ugly words others could hurl were a form of black magic. Like all spells, they were useless unless there was an opening. Words had to be taken personally to harm. They had to be believed on some level.

With Bless's self-acceptance came healing and slowly the ache in her tummy faded. She couldn't be harmed by a simple spell such as hurtful words. Even from the one she loved the most.

The silver Gateway Arch of Saint Louis was coming into view. The crystal, attuned to the light, blazed in the morning sun.

Rick felt fingers prodding him and digging into his pockets. Then he felt a sharp pain in his side as a foot connected with his ribs. He opened his eyes and saw sneakered feet running away. He turned his head toward the street and saw a police car cruising toward him.

A couple of minutes later, he felt the uniformed cops rolling him over. He knew it would behoove him to be unconscious, especially since he couldn't hear, so he kept his eyes closed.

He estimated it took fifteen minutes for him to be loaded on a stretcher. He couldn't wait to get to the hospital and some pens and paper.

Rick stared in astonishment and horror at the gibberish that was coming from his right hand. He could write, but nothing he jotted down made sense. He couldn't even write his own name.

Rick leaned back in bed, his eyes closed in momentary defeat. Those demons might be evil, but they weren't stupid.

The hospital personnel had run test after test. Since he couldn't hear, he had no idea of what the findings were. He'd finally been returned to his cubicle and he pantomimed writing. He'd been so relieved when they gave him a tablet of paper and a pen. He'd have somebody call Bless first thing. He knew that she'd come and get him and figure this thing out.

Now he was simply weary, unable to think of his next move. Apparently somebody was thinking for him, because two orderlies unlocked the brakes to his stretcher and wheeled him away to the elevator.

They took him to a locked ward and wheeled the stretcher into a barren room with two beds. Thankfully, he saw that both were empty. They moved him to a bed, lowered it, parked a wheelchair close, and provided him with some clean scrubs before they left him alone.

Rick struggled to stand up at the side of the bed. He lifted one leg, then another. That worked, but he couldn't place one foot in front of the other. Could he hop? Up and down in place. He couldn't hop forward or backward. He sighed and put on the scrubs, reached out, and pulled the wheelchair closer and eased himself down into it.

Suddenly, a memory of Bless's face hovered in front of him, as clear and crisp as if he could touch it. He missed her. Not simply to save his rear, although it did need saving, but he missed being around her. A day of not hearing her voice, smelling her scent, and feeling her touch had left a hollow within him. It was funny, but he didn't even remember feeling this way about Sharon. He'd loved Sharon, but it had a different texture altogether. A different kind of love.

This love he had for Bless was richer, more mature. Their love was new enough so the heat of infatuation still burned, but there was an underlying layer that made him know this was a woman he'd never tire of, a deep-down comfort that was addicting.

He didn't know what he'd do if Bless wasn't a part of his life. He couldn't bear another loss like Sharon. Life wouldn't be that cruel. But Bless had the most hazardous profession he ever heard of—demon slaying. Rick sighed again. He was both the luckiest and the unluckiest man in love that he could imagine.

Two women entered his room, both casually dressed in slacks and sweaters. One initiated rapid-fire signing gestures at him. Rick raised his shoulders and hands in the universal sign for "I don't know."

Their lips moved at him. Rick pointed to his ears. Can't hear, ladies, can't talk, can't walk, can't write, can't do crap.

After a while they left.

Rick tried to figure out how to get the woman who signed to teach him, or at least give him a book. He was going to figure out a way to communicate. That crazy heifer Ginger wasn't going to get the best of him.

The crystal led to a hospital. Bless drew in her breath sharply. Was he hurt? She glanced at the light in the crystal to reassure herself again that he was alive.

She headed for patient information. The pink-smocked gray-haired lady looked up with a smile. "May I help you?"

"I'm looking for a Rick Jensen. I believe he's a patient here."

The lady tapped the keyboard in front of her and peered at her computer screen. "No, I'm sorry, we don't have anybody with that name listed."

Bless bit her lip. "Uh, thanks."

She rounded a corner to get away from the busy lobby before she raised her crystal. It gleamed upward. She took the stairs.

By the time she reached the seventh floor, she was panting, sweating, and would swear she was about to have a heart attack. Bless leaned against a banister and took the crystal out. How many floors did this hospital have anyway? But to her extreme relief, the light shone on the exit door.

It led her to the psychiatric unit, a locked unit. Suppressing an urge to kick down the door, she asked the next person who unlocked the doors if she could speak to the nurse manager of the unit.

A few minutes later a harried-looking woman came out. "How can I help you?"

"I'm looking for somebody that I think is your patient, but he's not listed under his correct name. A black male, about six-two, medium-brown skin, clean-shaven, he was wearing jeans and a green polo shirt when he left home."

The nurse frowned. "And you are?"

Bless hesitated. If she said a friend, it would end right there. "I'm his wife," she said.

"Wait right here," the nurse said, and scurried through the door.

A few minutes later a man exited. "Hello, I'm Dr. Shearer. Ellen tells me that you have given the description of our John Doe and say you're his wife."

"Yes. May I see him?"

"He was found in north Saint Louis unconscious on the street. He had no ID on him."

"His name is Rick Jenson. He's a detective for the Atlanta Police Department. You can check."

The doctor raised his eyebrow. "That's a little hard to believe. This man is deaf, mute, and doesn't walk."

Bless closed her eyes momentarily. "Something must have happened to him. Please may I see him? At least see if it's him?"

The doctor shifted his weight from one foot to the other. "I don't see how it can hurt. Follow me."

31

Rick was sitting at the window in a wheelchair, bathed in the golden morning light. Bless rushed to him and fell across his lap, emotion overcoming her. She didn't know how afraid she'd been for him, until the relief that he was alive and well almost overwhelmed her.

She felt his arms lift her and she looked into his eyes, tender and brimming with happiness. He pulled her to him.

"So, I suppose that's settled. He obviously knows you. Our John Doe is ID'd," the doctor said.

Bless turned and blinked at the doctor, realizing that she was sitting on Rick's lap in the too-small wheelchair in the midst of a roomful of nurses and a doctor.

"Yes, this is Rick. I'll be out to sign any necessary papers, but could we spend a moment alone?" she asked.

The nurses were already leaving. "I'll see you in my office in a few minutes," the doctor said.

"Yes, I'll be there."

When the doctor first spoke, Rick didn't look in his direction. When they entered the room, four of them at once, he didn't move his head to see what was going on. The doctor said he couldn't hear or talk?

"Rick?" Bless asked, looking into his eyes.

He shook his head and pointed to his ears, and then he pointed to his tongue.

A spell, a heavy-duty one. And she had only a few minutes of privacy to lift it. She moved away from him and *looked* at him with that vision that was more than seeing. His aura was dampened by what looked like black bindings wrapping and strangling it.

Easier than she thought. She grabbed power and sent it to break the black bonds. It didn't touch them. She slammed against them with all she had, power enough to flame a battalion of demons, but they held.

Frustrated, she sank down on Rick's bed. He looked at her quizzically.

"I'm having trouble breaking the spell," she said.

He didn't even frown, but just relaxed his arms on the armrests and waited expectantly.

Bless knew he was trying to let her know that he had faith in her. Her mind raced, thinking of ways that the spell binding him could be broken.

She had an idea. From the inside. They might break from the inside, rather than being barraged by power from without. Black absorbed. She had a feeling that all the power she was sending from the outside merely strengthened the spell. After all, how were those spells cast? Through a chink on the inside, some gateway or weakness that allowed the spell to slip in. When he made the magic circle, it wasn't perfect. There must have been a tiny opening. Enough for the evil to slip in. The evil that he'd invited by the practice of magic.

She stood and approached him. "Rick, I want you to relax and breathe in and out, focusing on your breaths only."

He nodded and shut his eyes.

Bless stood behind him and touched his head with her palms. She couldn't strengthen another's aura enough to break bonds that tight. But he was her twin flame. Their power was meant to be shared. She closed her eyes and willed it to be so.

She felt something indefinable draining out of her and into him. The room felt as if it was spinning. Bless collapsed to the floor, weakened.

She struggled to her feet and went to stand in front of Rick. His eyes were wide and he was trembling slightly.

"Now, you can see, really see. See the glow around me?"

Rick hesitated, then nodded.

"That's my aura. Every object has one. It is the force that holds us together. The waves and colors in the room are transmission waves, radio waves, and the like. Ignore them. We don't have much time. I need you to look at your body, to perceive the black bonds that bind you. Do you see them?"

Rick looked down at his thighs, and nodded slowly.

"You need to break them yourself. You need to will it so. It will be as if your brain told your muscle to flex. Just want them gone."

Rick's eyes narrowed. His aura intensified and the new colors brightened. Suddenly the bonds snapped and withered into nothing.

Rick stood. "Thank you, love," he said, his voice hoarse from disuse.

She moved into his arms and he gathered her up. "What took you so long?" he whispered.

"A few demons. Traffic."

"Ahhhh," he said.

He kissed her lips, a tender and gentle touch. "Uh, Bless?"

"Yes?"

"How can you make all this stuff I'm seeing go away? I really don't like it."

Bless pulled away. "I gave you half my power. Your rightful half. I gave it back." She gave him a wicked grin. "Now you can fight demons too."

Rick frowned. "That means you are only half as strong."

"True, but now there are two of us. It should even out."

"No," Rick said.

"What?"

"No, I don't want this. Take it back."

She moved toward him and clasped his hands. "Remember when you wanted to help? Now you can. You're my equal in power. We can be a team."

"Bless, if it was meant to be like that in this life, I'd have had the power since birth. But for some reason, you had it all. Everything is for a reason; haven't you told me that?"

"Don't you want to be my equal?" Bless asked.

Rick stared at her. "I am your equal. Take your power back now."

"Hello?" A voice issued from the intercom on the wall. "The doctor is ready to see you. He's waiting."

"We need to take care of this," Bless said. "Let's go see the doctor together." She walked out of the room, feeling confused, conflicted, and a little hurt. Why didn't Rick appreciate her gift?

The doctor's eyebrows disappeared into his hairline when he saw Rick walk in. Rick's eyes dropped to the doctor's identification badge and he extended his hand. "Dr. Shearer," he said.

"I see you've made a miraculous recovery," the doctor said, his tone dry.

"We want to go home," Bless said.

Rick nodded. "I'd like to sign out."

Dr. Shearer leaned back in his chair. "That would be against medical advice."

"Fine. He'll sign," Bless said.

The doctor sighed. "All right. Why don't you two wait here while I have the nurse get the papers together for you to sign."

An hour later, they were walking out of the hospital. Bless noticed that Rick kept his eyes dropped. "There are ways not to perceive all that. To see what a normal person would see."

"This will be a moot point, because as soon as we're getting in the car, you're taking your power back."

They walked in silence to the car. Rick climbed into the passenger seat. Bless sat there for a moment, unmoving. "Tell me why the power is a bad thing?" she asked. "Think of all you can do, all you can learn."

"It's not what I'm supposed to do. You're always talking about having feelings, and now I feel it too. This is not my path. You need all your power and more to face what's ahead."

Bless sighed. "All right." She turned and took his hands. "Concentrate on the power you perceive in you flowing back to me." She drew the power, her power, out of him and felt it rushing home. Whew, that did feel better.

"Thank you," Rick said.

She smiled at him.

"Why do you think they dropped me off here? And why the elaborate spell? If they were going to let me live, wouldn't they have just let me walk away?"

"What the spell did was make it so you couldn't communicate, so you couldn't contact me. It made it harder for me to find you. If it wasn't for the crystal, it could have taken . . ."

They looked at each other in dawning realization.

"Glory," Bless said and she burned rubber peeling out of the parking lot.

"It's going to take seven or eight hours to drive. Take I-70 and head for the airport. I'll see if we can get on a plane."

"My cell phone is in my purse."

32

Nobody was answering the phone in Red Creek. Frantic, Bless called Mattie, a neighbor and a friend from church, and asked her to go over and check on Aunt Praise. The cell phone had been sitting on the airplane tray table for half an hour while Bless stared at it, willing it to ring and for Mattie to tell her that everything was fine.

The phone rang and Bless grabbed it.

"They aren't answering the door," Mattie said. "It's odd. Praise's car is in the garage, the lights are on, and I thought I heard a baby crying." Mattie paused. "Do you want me to call the authorities?"

"No, Mattie. I'm sure everything's all right and we'll be there in a few hours."

Bless clicked off after their goodbyes.

Rick was watching her. He intertwined his fingers with hers. "It will be all right," he said.

"Somehow I don't think so," Bless said.

"Everything will turn out all right in the end. That's what I think," Rick said.

Bless bit her lip and didn't answer.

The plane landed and they rushed straight to the rental counter to get a car. In twenty minutes they were on the highway, Rick speeding down the asphalt toward Red Creek.

"I feel like a fool," Bless said.

Rick turned down the radio to listen.

"I allowed myself to be manipulated and out-smarted by Ginger at every turn. All the time she wanted me out of the house and Red Creek, so they could make a strike at the baby. Do you real-ize what will happen if Glory is killed?"

Rick handed her a tissue. Bless had no idea tears were running down her cheeks. She wiped her eyes.

"It will be as if you lost your own child," Rick said quietly.

Bless sniffed. "Yes, it would. It would be hard to go on. But there's worse. Even if I leave out Glory's role at Armageddon and saving the whole freaking world, I'd be on the run and battling demons the rest of my life. Ginger won't rest until she kills me too. I'm next on her list, after Glory."

"We'll be on the run together, facing down the demons," Rick said.

"But you don't want to share my power."

"Bless, I'll always be at your side. I have my own sort of power."

Bless gazed at him. He meant it. He must have gone through some thinking like she did and had reached his own sort of epiphany. He was no longer worrying about her saving him, or besting him, but rather he radiated quiet confidence in the strengths he knew he had.

She liked it.

* * *

The sky deepened into dusk as Rick approached the house.

Bless moved into her other mode of seeing and gasped at the sight—the house was covered with demons. Demons trying to get in. The defenses were failing. Praise was under siege.

"Rick, demons are everywhere! It will look like I'm sitting here unconscious, but—"

"Go," he said.

She moved into the other plane and leapt through the metal of the car.

She whirled through the air to the house, screaming her battle cry and blazing violet fire.

Apparently her reputation preceded her, because the ranks of demons were already thinning, as they faded away and left. Demons weren't overly courageous creatures.

But there were enough left so the air was filled with lances of killing energy that were coming for her. She leapt in the air, twisting and evading them as she shot out energies of her own and fried a demon that looked something like a werewolf. A harpy demon descended and screamed as the violet flames caught her and burned her evil away. All that was left of her were a few ashes.

Bless ran toward the front door blasting demons in her path. She perceived Rick behind her. Since he belonged in the house, his entry would provide no opening for demons.

She ran through the door and dismay filled her. A few demons were already in the house. The wards shrieked. The defenses had been breeched, but had not completely failed yet. She heard Glory crying, but a snake-shaped demon blocked her way.

"Why don't you give up now?" it hissed. "I will make your death quick, I promise."

Bless sent a sheet of violet flame toward it. It met it with black energies and both were extinguished. There was a letter opener on the table by the foyer. She willed herself to be able to pick it up and she leapt in the air and landed on the snake's back. It writhed and twisted, trying to throw her off, its mouth open wide and its fangs dripping venom. She held on and inched her way up to its head. She grasped it around the neck and plunged the letter opener in its eye. The demon's screams shook the house as black gore poured out of its eye. She stabbed the other eye, and kept stabbing again and again, until the demon relaxed in death.

Bless jumped off the dead demon and ran toward Glory's room. Where was Praise? As she reached the stairs, she saw a still form lying at the top. Her stomach leaped toward her mouth, filling it with bitterness. It was Aunt Praise. Bless ran to her. Her aura still glowed, but was dimly fading.

"Aunt Praise," Bless called, kneeling beside her. She reached out to cradle her aunt, but her hands passed right through her.

"I did the best I could, Bless," Praise whispered. "I told you I was no demon slayer."

"Glory is still alive because of you," Bless said.

Praise smiled. "Yes, I did do something then, didn't I? Bye, now," she said, closing her eyes, and her aura faded completely away.

Bless choked back her emotions. She heard Glory's cry. There would be time for grief later.

She ran to Glory's room. For the first time she saw the blazing glory of the angels as they ringed the child, demon bodies at their feet.

Then her eyes narrowed. There was Ginger, darting toward the baby, knife drawn. "Ginger!" she screamed.

Ginger stopped, almost tripping over her own feet.

"Shit. Talk about showing up in the nick of time." She grinned. "And there's Rick. Bring him here."

A demon stood to the side of Ginger. It raised its tentacles, and before Bless could blast it, it shoved Rick toward Ginger. Bless blasted it to goo anyway, on general principles.

But Ginger had a dagger at the baby's chest. "And you, poor thing, aren't in the body. Rick, Bless is right there." Ginger pointed. "Looking stupid with her mouth hanging open because she can't do a damned thing to stop me."

Rick made a movement toward Ginger.

"Do you want this dagger in the brat's heart? Because if you don't make like a statue, that's where it'll be."

Rick froze.

Bless looked toward the angels. They shook their heads sadly. She knew that because of free will, they could not interfere directly. All they could do was guard the baby against demon attack. They were unable to do anything to Ginger, a living soul.

"I'm going to help you out, sis," Ginger said. "I'm going to give you a choice. Rick or the kid. You can't have both." She lowered the knife until it was resting on the baby's chest.

"Stop struggling, man. Haven't you figured out by now that my demon is holding you?"

Rick was trying to move and looking increasingly dismayed that he couldn't.

"Go ahead, Bless. Make up your mind. You have to ten. One—two—three—"

Bless willed herself to solidify and tried to rush Ginger. She went right through her.

It came down to this. Passion or duty. Didn't it always? There was only one choice to make, and it demanded a sacrifice she could hardly bear.

"Let Glory live," she said.

"I didn't hear you," Ginger said in a singsong voice.

She knew Rick couldn't see or hear her, but she approached him anyway. "Rick, it's the only thing to do. Our love will last through the ages."

Oh, screw this. "Ginger, you were always a sniveling coward. I dare you to step out and meet me face to face and settle this."

Ginger's eyes narrowed.

"Scared?" Bless said, her tone withering. "You were always so weak. Now you have your demons to do your bidding and you think that makes you hot stuff. But you are still nothing. And you look ugly as hell now too."

Ginger shrieked.

"C'mon, female dog. Let's take it outside. If you beat me, you have it all, Rick and the baby. Or were you too stupid to get that?"

"I'm gonna kill you!" Ginger yelled and left her body. Bless leaped up through the roof to the top of the house. Ginger followed, frothing at the mouth. Bless blasted the demons away and turned to meet Ginger in midair with her war cry. Ginger screeched and they leapt in the sky to meet, Ginger's fingers extended to claws, Bless's foot drew back to knock Ginger all up in her rear.

They went right through each other.

They settled on the roof, glaring at each other. "This isn't going to work," Ginger growled.

"No, it isn't," said Bless.

"Bless!" Rick called, his voice colored with alarm. Bless dropped through the roof back into Glory's room. Rick was still held by the demon, who was extending a tentacle to raise the knife, but every time he brought the knife up close to the baby, the angels would cut the tentacle off.

It must have looked to Rick as if the knife was jumping around on its own.

Bless noticed that the demon was not moving any closer toward the baby. The angels must have a range and the demon didn't want to be slain. Too bad.

Bless blasted the demon into black goop.

Rick, suddenly freed, darted toward Glory. But Ginger was there first, back in the body. She grabbed the dagger and held it at Glory's throat. "Uh, uh, uh," she said to Rick. He froze again, his eyes narrowed with anger.

"So it looks as if we're back to square one," Ginger said. She looked around. "Except I have no demons here. But no matter. Since you pissed me off so badly, Bless, I'm going to teach you a lesson. I'm going to kill both of them."

She raised her knife for the killing stroke, but Rick was quicker. He had her in a choke hold and bent the arm that was holding the knife behind her back.

"Let the knife go, or I'll break your arm."

Ginger dropped the knife but she was muttering words under her breath.

"Don't let her speak, Rick, she's casting a spell," Bless cried.

But of course he didn't hear her.

His eyes turned into a storm front when he realized that he couldn't move. Bless could see his muscles jerking as he strained.

"Bwa-ha-haaa," Ginger chortled, having perfected her evil laugh.

Rick was saying something. "You have no power over me," he said.

His muscles continued to ripple with exertion.

"You have no power over me," he repeated.

He was breaking free!

"You have no power over me."

His arms tightened at Ginger's throat and he dragged her away from the baby.

"You have no power over me."

Ginger gasped and gurgled as his fingers tightened.

"Rick!" Bless screamed. "You can't kill her, no!" He couldn't hear her, and his arm tightened against Ginger's throat, a red haze of hatred in his eyes.

Bless felt pure panic welling. If he killed Ginger, he would cross over to the darkness. He'd be working off the karma over lifetimes and they'd be separated. Again.

Then, as quickly as it came, Rick's rage evaporated. He dropped Ginger to the floor. "They have medication for people like you. And in the nuthouse where you'll be locked up for the rest of your life for murdering my brother, among others, there's plenty of it."

"Fool, this isn't over. You're going to die screaming at my hand," she said as she struggled to her feet.

She turned and darted to the windows. "Demons, catch me!" she screamed as she sailed through the glass. Bless and Rick rushed to the window. Bless saw the demons step aside as Ginger flew through the air and landed with a squish and crunch on the ground.

Rick inhaled sharply, grasped Glory, and rushed outside.

Bless followed, prepared to battle.

Rick took Glory outside where the demons congregated around Ginger's body. The angels blazed and happily commenced demon slaughtering. The rest of the demons scrambled to get out of Dodge, giving Bless a wide berth, she noticed.

Demons didn't like to die.

Rick touched Ginger's neck, and shook his head. He pulled out his cell phone.

Bless watched Ginger's spirit separate from her body. "Ginger," she called. "Go toward the light."

Then Bless saw it. A wash of light appeared near Ginger, a door, and she could see movement and colors beyond. Somebody was coming out.

A tall, slim woman with chiseled features, so dark she was almost black, emerged. She saw Ginger and smiled. "My child," she said.

Ginger's face lit up with joy. "Mama!" she cried.

Bless recognized her. Their mother, from when it all began on that hell boat bound for the Americas. So many lifetimes ago.

"I've been waiting for you. It's been so long," the woman said.

Miriam came out of the house. Bless started, having completely forgotten about her, and they both gazed at the woman.

She looked toward Bless and Miriam. "You've done well, my children. I'll finally see you soon."

Ginger was clinging to her, her face buried in her mother's neck. She moved with their mother into the light.

Miriam stood looking at the light until it faded and then turned and went back into the house, undoubtedly to watch some more television.

Then, an orb of light hung in the air with the suggestion of Malik's gun. Bless knew Rick saw it too, because he grinned back at it and said, "Later, bro." The light flashed and dissipated.

Bless moved back into her body and got out of the car. Rick ran to her with Glory and held them both in his arms.

After a moment Bless took Glory from him and held her soft against her chest as she leaned against Rick, his arm around her waist. They listened to the sound of sirens drawing closer. The circle was broken, and the wheel bearing the souls of the three slowed and came to a stop.

Epilogue

Rick walked toward Bless carrying a baby swaddled in a soft blanket, with Glory toddling at his side. He bent down and put their newborn son in her arms. Glory climbed on the bed beside Bless and leaned against her, sleepy. Rick sat on the other side, his arm around her, watching with a look of contentment on his face as Bless put their son to her breast.

New life at the end of days. The passing thought marred Bless's happiness. Rick read her expression. "The time is coming soon when things are going to change," he said. "But it's not the end; it's a new beginning of a wonderful world he'll grow up in, the dawn of a new age."

Rick was right. There was nothing to shadow their happiness. She reached out a hand and touched Rick's cheek, feeling Glory's warm body beside her and her dreamed-about and wished-for son at her breast. She'd been gifted with so much love her body could barely hold it in.

Bless kissed the top of her son's head and settled back into her husband's arms. They had the faith to see them through the coming trials and tribulations, and their love would last through the ages.

ABOUT THE AUTHOR

Monica Jackson is the author of eight novels, several novellas, short stories and essays. She is an award-winning author who lives in Kansas with her daughter.

Grab These Other
Dafina Novels
(mass market editions)

Check Out These Other
Dafina Novels

Sister Got Game
0-7582-0856-1

by Leslie Esdaile
$6.99US/**$9.99**CAN

Say Yes
0-7582-0853-7

by Donna Hill
$6.99US/**$9.99**CAN

In My Dreams
0-7582-0868-5

by Monica Jackson
$6.99US/**$9.99**CAN

True Lies
0-7582-0027-7

by Margaret Johnson-Hodge
$6.99US/**$9.99**CAN

Testimony
0-7582-0637-2

by Felicia Mason
$6.99US/**$9.99**CAN

Emotions
0-7582-0636-4

by Timmothy McCann
$6.99US/**$9.99**CAN

The Upper Room
0-7582-0889-8

by Mary Monroe
$6.99US/**$9.99**CAN

Got A Man
0-7582-0242-3

by Daaimah S. Poole
$6.99US/**$8.99**CAN

Available Wherever Books Are Sold!

Check out our website at www.kensingtonbooks.com.

Look For These Other
Dafina Novels

If I Could
0-7582-0131-1

by Donna Hill
$6.99US/**$9.99**CAN

Thunderland
0-7582-0247-4

by Brandon Massey
$6.99US/**$9.99**CAN

June In Winter
0-7582-0375-6

by Pat Phillips
$6.99US/**$9.99**CAN

Yo Yo Love
0-7582-0239-3

by Daaimah S. Poole
$6.99US/**$9.99**CAN

When Twilight Comes
0-7582-0033-1

by Gwynne Forster
$6.99US/**$9.99**CAN

It's A Thin Line
0-7582-0354-3

by Kimberla Lawson Roby
$6.99US/**$9.99**CAN

Perfect Timing
0-7582-0029-3

by Brenda Jackson
$6.99US/**$9.99**CAN

Never Again Once More
0-7582-0021-8

by Mary B. Morrison
$6.99US/**$8.99**CAN

Available Wherever Books Are Sold!

Check out our website at www.kensingtonbooks.com.

Your Five Senses and Your Sixth Sense

Hearing

Connor Dayton

PowerKiDS press.

New York

Published in 2014 by The Rosen Publishing Group, Inc.
29 East 21st Street, New York, NY 10010

First Edition

Editor: Jennifer Way
Book Design: Kate Vlachos

Photo Credits: Cover MIXA/Thinkstock; p. 4 KidStock/Blend Images/Getty Images; p. 7 Cynthia Kidwell/Shutterstock.com; p. 8 © Creatas/Creatas images/Thinkstock; pp. 11, 24 (ear) © iStockphoto.com/Aleksandar Zoric; p. 12 © Photodisc/David De Lossy/Thinkstock; p. 15 06photo/Shutterstock.com; pp. 16, 24 (hearing aid) Paul Matthew Photography/Shutterstock.com; p. 19 J5M/Shutterstock.com; p. 20 Kzenon/Shutterstock.com; p. 23 © Hemera/Thinkstock.

Library of Congress Cataloging-in-Publication Data

Dayton, Connor, author.
 Hearing / by Connor Dayton. — First edition.
     pages cm. — (Your five senses and your sixth sense)
 Includes index.
 ISBN 978-1-4777-3240-3 (library binding) — ISBN 978-1-4777-3242-7 (pbk.) — ISBN 978-1-4777-3239-7 (6-pack)
 1. Hearing—Juvenile literature. I. Title.
 QP462.2.D39 2014
 612.8'5—dc23
                              2013016411

Manufactured in the United States of America

CPSIA Compliance Information: Batch # W14PK3: For Further Information contact Rosen Publishing, New York, New York at 1-800-237-9932

CONTENTS

4

Hearing is one of your five senses. You use your **ears** to hear sound.

Sound is made of vibrations.
Every sound makes a
different vibration.

6

7

8

Sound moves in **waves**. Loud sounds make big waves. Quiet sounds make small waves.

Sound waves enter your ears. The sound waves vibrate parts in your ear.

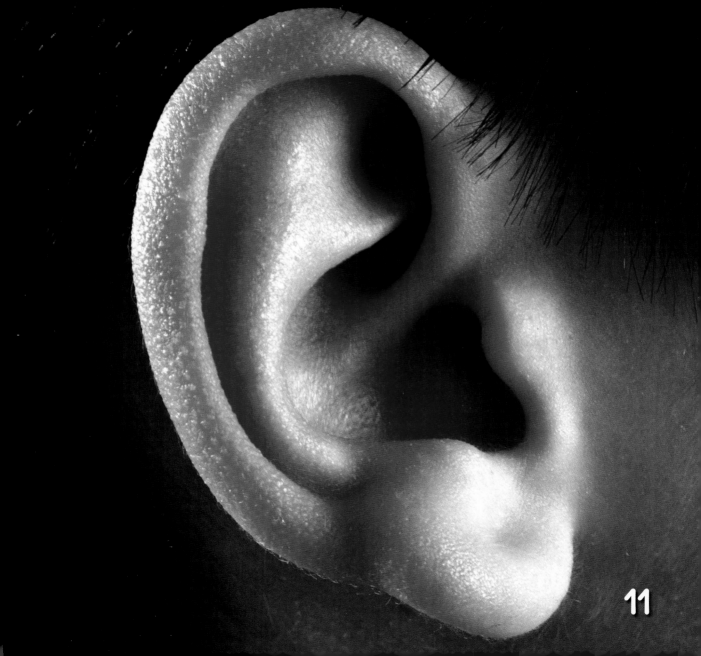
11

12

Nerves in your ears send signals to your brain. Your brain tells you what you hear.

Some sounds alert us.
We use units called decibels
to measure how loud
sounds are.

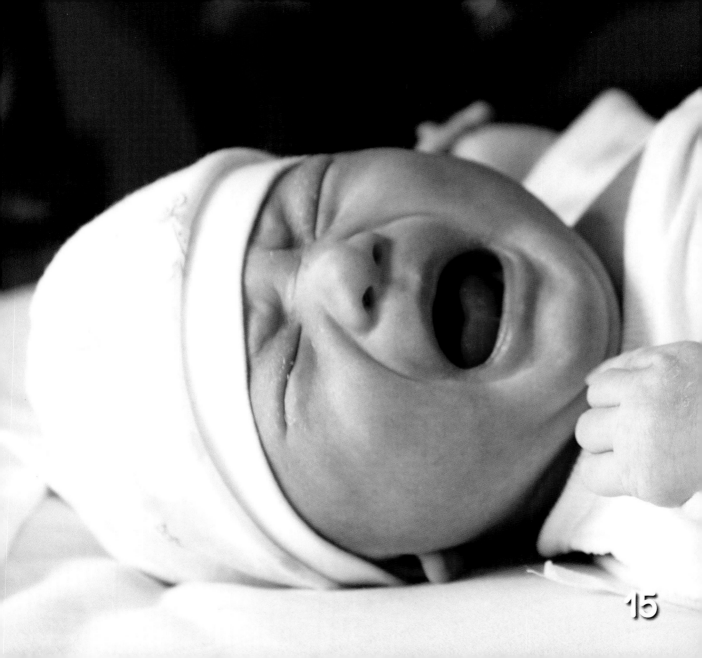

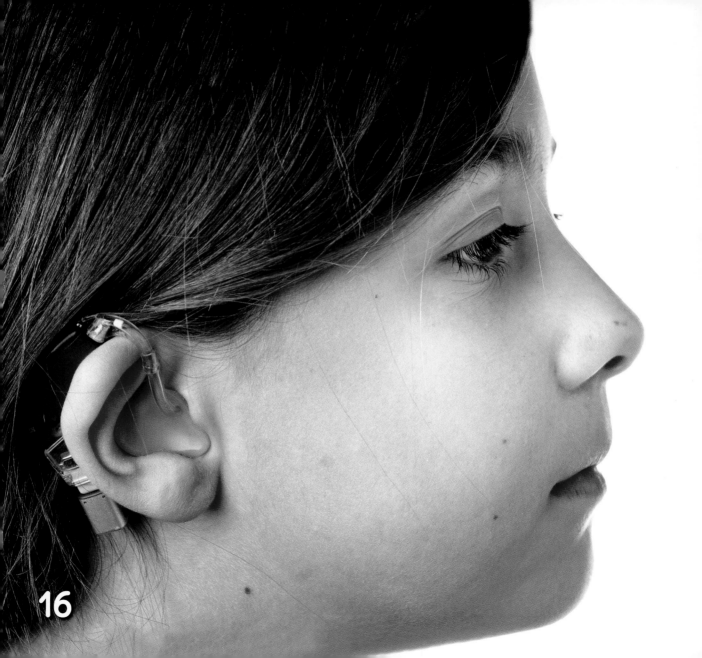

16

A person with poor hearing may use **hearing aids**. A person who is deaf cannot hear.

Loud noises can hurt your ears. This can cause hearing loss.

18

19

Keeping ears safe from loud sounds is smart. This can keep hearing loss from happening.

Hearing helps you learn about the world. What do you hear right now?

22

23

WORDS TO KNOW

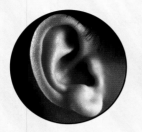

ear

hearing aid

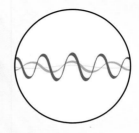

waves

WEBSITES

Due to the changing nature of Internet links, PowerKids Press has developed an online list of websites related to the subject of this book. This site is updated regularly. Please use this link to access the list:
www.powerkidslinks.com/yfsyss/hear/

INDEX